sands press
Brockville, Ontario

KRISTINA M. SERRANO

sands press

A division of 3244601 Canada Inc.
300 Central Avenue West
Brockville, Ontario
K6V 5V2

Toll Free 1-800-563-0911 or 613-498-2398
http://www.sandspress.com

ISBN 978-1-988281-24-7

Cover concept April Martinez
Formatting by Kevin Davidson & Renee Hare
Publisher Sands Press

1st Printing 2017
To book an author for your live event, please call: 1-800-563-0911

Submissions
Sands Press is a literary publisher interested in new and established authors wishing to develop and market their product. For more information please visit our website at www.sandspress.com.

DEDICATION

To Granddaddy, for introducing me to televised boxing matches.

ACKNOWLEDGEMENTS

Always first, I praise my Lord Jesus Christ. Also thanks to my parents, Roberto and Pamela Serrano, and family for listening to my constant dreams of becoming an author. To the amazingly professional team at Forever More Publishing for their hard work and thorough efforts in bringing SLOW ECHOES to life, especially Marisa Chenery for superb edits. To my beta readers, Heather Hofstetter, Ali Hodges and Mariah Wilson for your awesome critiques and priceless friendship. To more friends and talented writers, Sebastian Starcevic, Amber Forbes and Rachelle Shaw, for fantastic advice. To Mathew Weaver, Nolan Heath and Rebecca Haggist for sheer support and sweetness. To my BFF of half my life, Yvonne Wilson, for coaxing me out of pretty-pink-princess-picking-flowers mode. To Nina de Gramont. Your countless advice and support have meant the world to me. To Jason Mott for encouraging me to write a fourth book. To Margo Williams and Ann McCray for teaching me that "flowery" should describe a garden instead of words, and to Lee Cannon, Livingston Sheats, Tim Bass and all my other wonderful teachers who helped shape my writing and publishing knowledge over the years.

SITE ONE: SNOW HILL, MARYLAND

CHAPTER ONE

The domino effect—one person trips, several people fall. Especially my family. When it came to falling, we didn't have a choice. If we wanted to stay alive, people had to fall with us.

Tonight, I had no clue, even when one guy's stumble knocked a whole crowd forward.

"You're a jerk, Casebolt!" a man yelled into the stunned silence. "I hope Wilkinson beats you to a pulp!"

A young guy laughed, his silky voice out of place in the room of beer-filled men and blood. "Yeah, you wish, Appleton." Appleton. He'd just won the heavyweight rounds. "And your mom wishes she'd left you at the hospital after you were born."

Appleton shouted something else, and in the cool light of the wine-bottle chandeliers, I saw a couple men scrape a guy off the floor. He then proceeded to push his way through the crowd, lifting his hands to put gloves on as he went.

"Coming, ref," he called, the men shifting as if he were a mole tunneling beneath the earth. "Don't start the fight without me."

I only saw bits of him as he walked toward the ring—a flash of ashen skin here or there, a glimpse of messy wheat-colored hair.

He disappeared as he climbed through the ropes. The first thing I noticed was the ticked look the referee gave him, complete with crossed arms. The second thing was his purple-black right eye.

The third thing I noticed was him.

He raised his long, sculpted arms to the ceiling to stretch, a tattoo circling his left biceps in a frayed loop. After rolling his head a couple times, he said to the referee, "What? I'm here, aren't I? Let's get this show on the road."

"Get in your corner, Casebolt."

1

Casebolt knocked gloves with Wilkinson—who was just as if not more ticked than the referee—before obeying the command.

Something was odd about this last fight. I couldn't put my finger on it until I saw Wilkinson's corner man clinging to the rope behind him, waiting to rinse out his mouth and wipe sweat and blood from his face after each round. Casebolt had no one.

"Shouldn't he have someone in his corner?" I glanced at Casebolt, who slipped in his mouth guard.

"Yeah, he should," Cliff, my boxing and kickboxing instructor, said, "but he's the black sheep of the boxing community. Guess no one wanted the task."

"But *someone* could stand in," I protested, turning to Cliff. "No matter how jerky, every fighter needs someone in his corner."

The referee was just announcing the start of the first round when Sheridan, Snow Hill's professional flirt and beefy instructor for advanced fighters, patted my shoulder. "You're right, honey. I'll grab a towel. He's my new roommate, after all."

I hadn't realized I'd been holding my breath until I let it out when Sheridan left, pushing his way to the edge of the ring. He climbed up the side and then said something to Casebolt, who nodded, before disappearing as the referee rang the bell.

Wilkinson was obviously older and more experienced, not to mention looked as if he was pushing heavyweight. As the two circled one another, the larger man's gaze was intense and focused while the younger contender seemed almost bored. As if he wanted to get hit, Casebolt's gloves weren't as high as they should have been. He held them by his bellybutton. To my surprise, he was the one to make the first move—a jolting jab, then cross to the jaw that reminded me of a baseball bat striking a ball at full force.

"I'm not sure who to call on this round," Cliff said into my ear.

I turned my head, but didn't take my gaze off the ring. "Are you kidding me?" Casebolt landed a few more jabs before Wilkinson was able to make contact, and that was just a graze against the shoulder.

Sheridan returned as the first round ended. Casebolt ambled over to him, a bored look on his face. He didn't even sit on his stool in the corner or get a sip of water, just halfheartedly blotted his face with the towel

Sheridan had handed him and then walked back to the middle of the ring. Glaring, the referee said something to him that sent him to his corner to start the next round.

As he stepped across the canvas, walking closer to my side of the ring this time, he did a double take. His gaze held mine for only a moment, but it felt like so much longer. Curiosity danced between us, so many questions neither of us could ask. *Or can I?*

I'd come there because I'd wanted to watch live fights, but also because I'd chosen to do my senior project on boxing. Now I knew who I wanted to interview for my article.

Wilkinson only made it to round three before Casebolt knocked him out cold. I'd seen it, but I really couldn't believe it. It wasn't as if Wilkinson hadn't been trying. It wasn't as if he didn't have a billion times more experience than this guy. No cheating, no foul play. Just sheer good punching.

I struggled to keep my gaze on Casebolt as the announcer declared the end of the fights, and the crowd began to break up, but I lost him the moment he stepped down from the ring.

Cliff tapped my shoulder. "Let's wait here until most of this crowd is gone. It'll be easier to get out that way."

I bit my lip, glancing back at the ring. Cliff would probably be more than happy to help me track down the boxer of my choice for my interview, but, for reasons I couldn't explain, I didn't want him to go with me. *So how do I ditch him and Sheridan long enough to track down Casebolt? Sheridan...*

I glanced beside me. Sheridan walked away, talking to a couple men in the crowd. "Okay," I said to Cliff. "I just want to ask Sheridan something really quick."

I darted across the short distance through the remaining crowd before Cliff could follow.

The two men and Sheridan arched their brows at me when I smacked him on the shoulder. "Where's the locker room?"

He jerked his chin at the wall behind me. "Back left corner, as soon as you come into the room." Grinning, he said, "You got an eye on one of the boxers?" I didn't reply, just muttered a quick "thanks" and whirled around.

Shutting the door behind me, I took a deep breath before turning the corner, scanning the room for Casebolt. All the other boxers had apparently left. Only Wilkinson sat on the bench by his locker, looking up at my approach, his face distorted and puffy from Casebolt's relentless fists.

He smiled. "I knew I couldn't have gotten hit *that* hard. Thought I saw a beautiful woman out there."

I kept my face as indifferent as possible, trying to be businesslike. "Is Casebolt here? I'd like to have a word with him." I pulled out my notepad and pen for emphasis.

Wilkinson's expression hardened. "I don't know how the owner of this place would feel about reporters snooping around. He wants to keep it hushed. Not that he's doing anything illegal."

I thought fast. "Oh, I'm not interested in the place. The name will be left out completely. I only need to interview a boxer for my…article."

Wilkinson shrugged. "Don't see any harm in that." He glanced over his shoulder. "Since Casebolt isn't around, maybe you'd like to interview a *real* contender."

"If I'm not mistaken, Casebolt just creamed you out there." Not wanting to belittle Wilkinson's supposed talent, I added, "But congratulations on your twenty-four knockouts. I'm sorry to see your perfect score broken."

Wilkinson glared, then shrugged it off. "It was bound to be broken sooner or later." After a pause, he said, "You know, you've got a lot of guts to come in here."

I glanced behind me at the wall covering the door, expecting Cliff to walk in at any minute. "So has Casebolt left already or not?" I asked, not wanting to waste more time.

"Nope. Just about to hit the showers."

My gaze shot toward the entrance to the showers. Casebolt stepped through the open space, wearing only a towel and a curious expression. I swallowed hard. My inexperience threatened to leak through my composure, but I fought it back. For now, I was a collected reporter who was strictly business. That was what I kept telling myself.

He studied me intently, probably wondering, like everyone else, why I was there. "If this guy's bothering you, I can knock him out. Again."

He wasn't smiling, but there was a smug glint in his eyes as he glanced at Wilkinson.

"How about I give you another black eye to match the one Appleton gave you?" Wilkinson stood and stalked off, muttering, "I'd bet fifty bucks she'll give up on the interview and give him a black eye herself."

Once Wilkinson was out of sight, I closed the distance between myself and Casebolt and extended my hand, my mind racing from fast thinking. "Pleased to meet you, Mr. Casebolt. I'm on assignment for the *Riverwood Chronicle* and would be grateful if you'd spare a few minutes for an interview."

He blinked, taken aback, but replied swiftly. "Sure. I've got nothing better to do." Shifting his weight, he added, "Call me Whistler."

I smiled, fighting back my paranoia about the door opening. "Great." After undoing the cap on my pen, I flipped open my notebook and skimmed through my questions, quickly realizing none of them did him justice. Looking back at him, I decided to let my curiosity guide me through the interview. "First of all, where did you learn to hit like that? And at such a young age. I presume you're eighteen, nineteen?"

He laughed. "Twenty-one. And I learned from the Internet." When he saw no amusement in my expression, he said, "Honestly, I just get frustrated a lot, and punching something seems to calm me down, so I've had a lot of practice."

"Okay...I'll just put that you're a natural." I didn't know why, but I believed him. "There seems to be a lot of tension between you and your fellow contenders. Would you describe yourself as the 'black sheep' of the ring?"

He looked at me strangely before answering, and I immediately regretted the question. Too personal. I didn't know how real reporters did it.

"Yeah," he said, almost proudly. I was relieved he was more intrigued by my boldness than anything else. "Black sheep with a black eye. Appleton caught me off guard. Actually, the fights before the fights are usually more fun."

I asked him a few more significant questions, but during the rest of the interview, I still couldn't figure out what I really wanted to ask. What had prompted me to ditch Cliff and dart into a men's locker room?

"So what do you see in your future?"

He gave me a strange look, accompanied by a smug smile, as if he'd hidden an important key no one knew existed. "None of us can see more than a few yards out, now, can we?" He glanced at the wall behind me.

Two seconds later, the door opened and shut, and Cliff stepped around the partition.

I glanced at Whistler, furrowing my brows at the coincidence, but figured he just had good hearing.

"Hey," I said, walking to Cliff, "I just finished interviewing the subject. Ready to leave?"

"Fellow reporter?" I turned back to Whistler, who eyed Cliff curiously.

Biting the inside of my mouth, I remembered that this wasn't the first time the two had seen each other, so I went with the truth. "Personal trainer."

"I can tell you work out," Whistler said, though he kept his gaze on my face, which surprised me.

I smiled and walked back to him, offering my hand. "Thank you for your time. And keep up the good fights."

He shook my hand quickly, but held it still a second before letting go. "Thanks, Miss…"

"Baioumi. Selk Veronika Baioumi."

He narrowed his eyes in surprise. "Selk. That's Egyptian, right? Some kind of prefix or something of the goddess Isis?"

"Yeah, sort of," I said, the surprised one now. It was fairly common knowledge for anyone who'd taken classes or read books on archaeology or mythology, but Whistler just didn't strike me as that type of guy.

"We need to get going, Selk."

Cliff's flat voice jostled me from my thoughts. Glancing at him, I noticed a lack of emotion on his face. I groaned internally. The car ride home would be one big speech with no discussion of the boxing matches.

I nodded and headed toward the door, pausing to face Whistler once more. "Thanks again for your time."

"No prob. Maybe I'll see you around the gym."

My stomach twisted at that thought. I'd never seen him there before.

His workout schedule must have been during my school hours. I wondered how he was outside the ring, how he practiced on the punching bags. And what would such a gifted fighter think of me, a teenage girl, who'd never been in a match? Would he find my skill impressive or my punches weak? Why did I even freaking care?

I figured it'd be better to play it safe, at least for a while. For now, I wouldn't tell him about my age or boxing hobby. I'd just be Reporter Selk Baioumi from the *Riverwood Chronicle*, who liked to keep fit at the gym.

"Yeah," I said with a small smile. "Maybe."

Cliff grabbed my hand and pulled me away, glaring at Whistler as he led me through the door. He didn't stop until we'd reached the bottom of the staircase that led out of Man Cave, which was all but empty now.

"You just *had* to pick the scummiest guy here for your interview," he said. "I probably wouldn't have even brought you if I'd known he was going to be here."

"He may have an edgy personality, but he's not scum. In fact, I'd call him nice."

Cliff looked at me, his expression one of disbelief. "You've never been this naïve, Selk. Not even Sheridan knows anything about the guy, where he's from. Serial killers can be 'nice.' And that was the first time I've ever seen fake civility from him."

Pouting a little, I wondered aloud, "So does that mean you won't bring me back?"

"No," Cliff said, sighing. "You look older than seventeen, so smuggling you in here isn't hard. Just be careful introducing yourself to strange men, okay?"

I pushed past Cliff, not wanting to discuss it further. He was kind of right. Whistler Casebolt was everything I usually ignored or just didn't notice, but there was something about him, something that told me he had a reason for the way he acted.

This interview wasn't over. It was only beginning.

CHAPTER TWO

Light Hooks

The Egyptology Gazette

Breaking News!

Eye of Horus Amulet Taken Off Exhibit at the British Museum in London, England

Due to several attempts made to steal the artifact, it has been removed from display and placed into a secure storage chamber inside the museum, the location not to be released to the public.

What puzzles staff and officials the most is that the other artifacts remained untouched, only the alarm by the amulet's case having been triggered.

Some have suggested an extreme archaeology enthusiast to be the culprit, but this leaves yet another question unanswered. The Eye of Horus was a common symbol in ancient Egypt, supplying museums with several artifacts bearing its image, a few still on display in The British Museum. If this is the case, what makes this amulet so coveted?

I'd just applied to several colleges for the fall in hopes of being accepted into their archaeology and Egyptology programs—boxing was only one of my passions. I liked to keep track of the latest Egyptology discoveries, but although this article was intriguing, the writer's attempt to bull-crap around the fact that no one had any real evidence bored me.

I closed my laptop and scooped up Tut, my Egyptian Mau cat, AKA a long-ago birthday present from my grandpa. He'd been the one to get me into boxing, telling me I needed to take lessons when I got old enough so I could protect myself.

When he died just before my twelfth birthday, I gave myself time to recover before deciding to honor his request. That was when I found Cliff, his black hair, blue eyes and peaches complexion convincing my friends that he was Elvis reincarnated. He was only twenty, and had just moved to Snow Hill. After two small fights, he'd realized that he didn't like the . intensity and pressure of competition, and would rather teach what he'd learned from his career-boxer dad.

It was Cliff who'd pricked my interest in kickboxing. I'd seen him watching a match on a gym TV one day while he waited for me to show up for my lesson. I was fourteen when I added that to my workout list, and shortly after I turned fifteen, he stopped charging me for sessions because he said I was starting to feel more like an opponent instead of a student.

Whistler sure wasn't a student.

So much for a distraction. I'd been so overwhelmed the night before, I'd instantly fallen asleep. Now my pondering picked back up. I'd never understood girls who were always like, "There's just *something* about him," whenever being drawn to a particular guy. After meeting Whistler, I did. There *was* just something about him. I couldn't think of a better way to put it, because I couldn't pinpoint anything.

Maybe punching something would help me sort my thoughts out.

I found Cliff and Sheridan in the back of the gym. After tossing my gym gear aside, I darted to Cliff's side and slammed the bag, sending it bouncing into his and Sheridan's chins.

"Good morning, fellas. What a fine day for punching things just for the heck of it."

Cliff laughed and rubbed his chin once the annoyed expression left his face. "I didn't expect to see you so early today after last night."

Sheridan winked at me and ran a hand through his shoulder-length, milk-chocolate hair. "Don't you ever get tired of sweaty gyms?"

"Nope," I said, punching the speed bag again, lightly this time. "You two got many students today?"

"I've got one at noon and Sheridan has two this afternoon. Otherwise, no. Slow day."

"Great," I said, grinning. "Then maybe you guys can help me finish my senior project. One interview isn't enough."

"So that's where you disappeared to last night," Sheridan commented, smirking and crossing his arms. "And probably why you're uncharacteristically giddy today. You've got your eye on one of the boxers."

I bit my tongue, trying to distract myself from blushing.

"She has a thing for Bateson." Cliff winked at me now, reminding me of the winner I'd called on a lightweight round at Man Cave the night before.

I would have decked him if I hadn't been so grateful that he and Sheridan weren't aware of how strong an effect Whistler had had on me.

Instead, I walked to my gym bag to get my notepad and pen, deciding a couple more interviews for my senior project wouldn't hurt. "Very funny, but enough lies about me. I want to record some facts about you."

When I finished, Cliff just stared.

"What?" I asked.

"For a girl of action, paper and words is a pretty boring senior project."

I crossed my arms, curious. "What do you mean?"

His lips lifted into a slanted smile as he glanced around the boxing corner of the gym. "This is supposed to be about your hobby. Your teachers would be impressed if they saw how seriously you took your own training."

I shrugged. "I don't take my training seriously. I do it for fun. I'm no professional."

"You're talented. Your teachers should see proof of your passion for your topic."

I pressed my lips together. "Does your phone have a video camera?"

"Yeah. The quality's not too terrible."

"Great," I said, shrugging out of my jacket. "You can e-mail the videos to me."

I did a warmup demonstration and then beat up several of the punching bags.

"Nice, honey," Sheridan said, clapping.

"Do you think the speed bag, jumping rope and a few punches are enough?" I asked. "Shouldn't I actually fight someone?"

Cliff frowned. "You know how I feel about you getting hit by one of us."

"You can beat me up, honey," Sheridan volunteered. "Unrequited punches."

Cliff shrugged.

"All right," I said, turning back to Sheridan. "You know, I may have practiced with you a couple times, but I don't think I've had the privilege of seriously punching you yet."

Sheridan bowed and gestured toward the ring. "After you, honey."

Readjusting my gloves, I stepped into the ring, curious about how this would go. Sheridan was massive. I feared I wouldn't be able to do any damage, but Cliff's no-hitting-Selk rule gave us each an advantage—I could throw all my energy into punching, and Sheridan could throw all his into blocking.

It took a while, but a few combos and a couple hooks finally sent him into the ropes.

"Dang, go, Selk!" Cliff called, and the video camera beeped. Hmm… Off camera.

Before Sheridan could right himself, I charged him with a series of kicks, finishing him off with a spinning blow that made my ankle vibrate. Sheridan, meet canvas. Canvas, Sheridan.

He lay still in shock. I took off a glove and then offered him a hand. He took it and shook it, glancing at Cliff as he stood. "You sure you shouldn't upgrade to pro trainer?"

Cliff shrugged. "Selk's exceptionally talented. I thought I warned you."

Rubbing his jaw, Sheridan was about to say something else when clapping came from somewhere beside the ring.

"Wow."

Tensing, I faced the owner of the familiar voice. He leaned against the ropes, looking as if he'd just woken up not too long ago.

"I thought you had a personal trainer, not a boxing instructor." He glanced at Cliff. "Did *he* teach you that, or did my roommate coach you?"

Roommate? My mind blanked for a second before I remembered. Sheridan and Whistler were roommates. How could I have forgotten?

Clearing my throat to avoid a high-pitched voice, I said, "Cliff's been training me for years. Sheridan just volunteered to get beaten up."

Whistler laughed dryly. "I can see that." After pulling himself into the ring, he crossed the canvas and stopped a foot away from me, studying my eyes. "Ever thought of going pro?"

My heart fluttered at his words. I hadn't realized how badly I'd wanted to impress him until he'd said them. "No. This is just for fun. I have other career plans."

"Like working for a magazine." He narrowed his eyes and crossed his arms in doubt.

Giving him a mysterious half smile, I said, "Something like that." I dared to hold his gaze a full four seconds—I counted—before walking out of the ring and then stripping off my other glove.

"So, what's the camera for?" he pressed, leaning over the ropes. "To go with your article?"

Sheridan arched his brows. He must not have known who I'd interviewed.

I bit my lip. My mind worked fast. "To watch myself so I can see where I need to improve."

Whistler smiled a sultry smile. "There isn't much you could improve on. If you really want to, you need to practice more blocking and dodging instead of just hitting."

I wanted to hug him, for a bunch of reasons, but mostly because of his comment. Throwing an exasperated look at Cliff, I said, "Thank you! Finally, someone other than *me* says it."

Cliff glared at him. "I've covered plenty of defense with Selk."

"Has she practiced?" Whistler pressed, winking at me in a teamwork kind of way that didn't annoy me or creep me out.

"No," I chimed in. "I haven't."

Whistler lifted the ropes and gestured toward the ring. "Then come on. You and me, right here, right now."

He threw me a challenging smile I couldn't resist. My gloves were back on and I was in the ring before I knew it.

"Sheridan, if you would kindly depart," Whistler said without taking his gaze off me.

Sheridan shrugged and stepped out of the ring. "Your call, man. It's up to you if you want to get beaten up by a girl."

"No way." Cliff pocketed his phone and stepped between Whistler and me. "As part of the gym staff, I have the authority to keep gym rules in check. Men do not hit women." He glanced at me. "Especially Selk."

He looked at Sheridan for support, but Sheridan just shrugged again. "I really think she can hold her own, man."

"Stop acting like a pompous dork," I said. "You know those are *your* rules, not the gym rules."

"You don't know that," Cliff countered. "I could have a no-hitting-Selk sign hung by the ring in a heartbeat."

Whistler walked up behind me. His willowy shadow stretched over Cliff. "Relax. I promise if anyone gets hurt, it'll be me. Trust me."

Cliff gave him a look that told him he'd never trust him in a million years, but after seeing the determination in my eyes, he sighed and stepped down from the ring. "If you hurt her, you're dead."

"Fair warning," Whistler said, then returned to the center of the ring. When I joined him and took position, he held up a hand and looked at Cliff. "Still got that camera? She'll want to watch this."

I certainly would. Glaring, Cliff reluctantly withdrew his phone from his pocket and began videoing.

Deciding not to waste time, I went for his face, but he blocked the jab. "Too early," he said, jogging around me.

When he lashed at me with a return jab, I was taken aback, partly because it felt as if I was really fighting for the first time in my life, and partly because his ungloved fist should have knocked me to the floor. Though every movement of the punch was proper, his knuckles barely brushed my face. I got it now. He'd teach me how to block in a touch-not-tackle-football kind of way.

Why hadn't Cliff ever done that with me?

"Feel free to beat me up, just like Sheridan," he said as we continued circling. "I'm a fast healer."

My jaw dropped a little in realization when he said that, but I made myself recover so the camera wouldn't catch my shock. He'd had a serious black eye last night, but now it was gone.

"You mean you turn into a drag queen and wear makeup to cover up those black eyes," Sheridan sneered, as if reading my thoughts.

I squinted. There may have been just a trace of purple left, but still. I didn't see how any amount of makeup could have covered up that bruise.

"Well, maybe Selk will give me another one to add to my secret collection."

After blocking a series of jabs, I landed three punches in a gut-face-gut combo that sent him stumbling backward. We blocked and replied to each other a few more times before I sent Whistler into the ropes again with another combo.

Sheridan rang the bell, declaring the end of the unique fight. I would have used the same kickboxing moves to finish him, but as much as I wanted to impress him, part of me was as hesitant to hurt him as he was to hurt me. That freaked me out.

Whistler bounced off the ropes and jogged to me, then shook my gloved hand. "Well done. For a reporter, you're good at blocking."

Wish I could say the same about reporting.

"Thanks for the sparring session," I said. "I thought you'd be taking a break from the gym after creaming Wilkinson last night."

"My energy is endless," he said, keeping my gaze.

"Selk?"

"What?" I blinked and turned around.

"I asked you a question," Cliff said, climbing into the ring.

"Sorry. What was it?"

"Do you want to grab breakfast at Mack's Shack while we're not too sweaty and then come back for my student's lesson?"

The local favorite eatery was five blocks from the gym and three blocks from my house. Mack was like Santa without a beard, couldn't keep a sour face if he tried. Rumors floated around that he had a huge crush on Mom, but he was a little too old for her, and she hadn't seen anyone since Dad had left.

Torn, I glanced at Whistler. "I guess. Unless Whistler cares to show me what he's got on the canvas bag. I feel like he was holding out on Wilkinson last night, and he definitely held out on me just now."

Whistler actually grinned. I couldn't remember seeing him grin. "Since I'm warmed up now, why not?"

Glancing at Cliff, I suggested, "Why don't you and Sheridan go have bro time or something? I don't usually eat this early, anyway."

"Same," Whistler commented, slipping through the ropes of the ring. "I'm a lunch guy."

Cliff opened his mouth as if to protest, but Sheridan beat him to it. "Come on, man. She's in good hands." I thought I heard him add, "For fighting, at least."

Cliff hesitated, then muttered something under his breath and left the ring. "We'll be right back," he called as Sheridan shoved him through the gym.

Breathing a sigh of relief, I hopped down from the ring and then jogged to Whistler. My stomach fluttered as if finally hatching long-cocooned butterflies.

"You sure he's just your trainer? He's way protective of you."

I rolled my eyes. "He can be a pain, but he's like my brother. In those cases, you learn to put up with annoying things."

"If you say so."

"Well," I added, following him to the swinging canvas bag, "you kind of have a reputation. At least within the boxing community. Though I don't see…"

He swung a couple light hooks at the bag and glanced at me. "Don't see what?"

Since I could find no way around the word… "I don't see where you're an impossible jerk like everyone says."

He faced me, the corner of his mouth twitching with a frail smile. "Then maybe they're the jerks, and you and I are the only normal ones."

Normal. "Speaking of which," I said, stepping closer to the bag, "was Sheridan joking about the makeup?"

"What do you think?" He landed a few more punches on the canvas.

"I think that's the only way your black eye could disappear."

He muttered something, then smirked and pummeled the bag with knockout blows, and kept it up for at least five minutes. I admired him in silence, almost forgetting the subject.

Not even panting and still gloveless, he said, "There are more ways to make a black eye disappear than you think." I was about to comment when he added, "Your turn."

Furrowing my brows, but deciding to let it go, I started off on the bag with light punches as he had, then morphed to my hardest hits, and finished with a series of kickboxing combos I couldn't resist.

"Nice," Whistler said in approval. "Maybe Cliff knows a thing or two about fighting, after all."

"He's better than I give him credit for," I admitted, only a little irritated that I was still trying to catch my breath when Whistler hadn't even broken a sweat.

Whistler stayed silent for a while, studying me. Then, he said out of nowhere, "Egyptian, huh?"

I blinked, taken aback. "Yeah. Well, my dad was. My mom's Croatian."

Whistler smiled a genuine smile. "I was born in Croatia to American parents. And, even more ironically, I was shipped to the U.S. and fostered by Egyptian-Americans when I was a baby."

My jaw dropped. What else could this guy possibly have in common with me? "Seriously? Where are they now? Your foster parents, I mean."

He shrugged. "Don't know. Dead, I guess. Or maybe they moved back to Egypt. They were into artifacts and stuff." He smiled a slanted smile. "Selk. It's funny that meeting you wasn't the first time I heard that name. I'm surprised my foster parents didn't rename me Horus or Tutankhamen."

I laughed. "My cat is an Egyptian Mau—named Tutankhamen. A present from my grandpa, on my Croatian side." Frowning, I pressed, "You really don't know what happened to your foster parents?"

"Nope. All I remember is them forcing me out of the house when I was fourteen after they caught me checking out one of their artifacts. My memory's a bit blurry in spots before that. I'm not really sure what happened, but it had to be more than punishment for going through their stuff out of boredom." His eyes widened a little, as if he hadn't anticipated telling me that much, and then he shook his head. "Your dad dead too?"

"Don't know. He left the day after I was born." I'd never even seen his picture, but I knew my pale latte skin, black eyes and dark-chocolate hair hadn't come from Mom. "I've got my mom, though." My gaze clutched Whistler's for the longest time. For so long I didn't hear Cliff and Sheridan approach until they were inches away.

"Switched from sparring sessions to staring contests?" Sheridan teased.

I averted my eyes, but Whistler's gaze held on for a moment more before he replied to Sheridan. "No. Just taking a break. We both just tortured the canvas bag." He swung his arms and rocked on his heels. "I should go."

Ignoring Sheridan and Cliff, he smiled the smallest smile over his shoulder at me as he left. "You coming to Man Cave again Friday, Selk?"

I glanced at Cliff and Sheridan. They'd gotten me in last time. "Well, it's a men's-only hangout, so it's up to these guys whether or not they want to smuggle me in again."

"I can get you in."

"If you don't get kicked out first," Cliff commented, coughing sarcastically.

"That shouldn't be a problem," Whistler said, glaring at him. "I'm refereeing."

"You're refereeing?" Sheridan repeated in disbelief.

"Yep. Filling in. No one else was willing to give up their fights."

I grinned. "I definitely can't miss this."

He smiled that dry smile again. "Catch you later."

"Catch you later," I said, my voice soft.

Once he'd gone, Sheridan whistled. "Heavy. What were you two talking about?"

I frowned, my mind unable to make sense of our conversation. "Egyptian and Croatian things. Parents. I really don't know. You guys ate fast." Or maybe hanging out with Whistler had made time fly.

Did he, however mild, really have amnesia?

CHAPTER THREE

One Place

The Egyptology Gazette

Breaking News!

Artifact Theft

Despite extreme security measures, the inexplicably coveted Eye of Horus amulet has been stolen! The event is thought to have taken place after three a.m., London time.

Word is that not only did the thief somehow manage to distract security, dismantle cameras and lasers and open a bulletproof glass box, but he or she also resealed it and reset the lasers and cameras before security knew what had happened.

This is one of the most perplexing and skilled thefts of our time. Perhaps Sherlock Holmes himself would hesitate before tackling such a mystery. Other than how, there still remains the museum's (and the public's) most pressing question—why?

Updates to follow as received.

I scoffed at my laptop, not expecting to find that Monday morning. I'd spent the rest of Saturday and all of Sunday at home, catching up with Mom and Tut and beginning to organize my senior project, AKA, watching reruns of my sparring session with Whistler. There was something so sincere about him, something, I gathered, very few people looked close enough to see.

Friday night, he looked nothing like a referee in his jeans and orange hoodie. The boxers rolled their eyes at him as he grabbed the megaphone hanging on one of the ropes. Instead of pumping up the audience, he just glanced between the two boxers, both heavyweights, in the ring. "Hook and jab, but don't screw each other over."

"In other words, don't do what you would do," the boxer to my left snarled. Appleton.

"Hey," Whistler countered, still speaking into the megaphone, "I've never hit below the belt or thrown rabbit punches. In the ring, that is." A few men in the audience actually laughed at that. "Round one," he concluded, then rang the bell.

As much as I hated to admit it—especially to Cliff—I couldn't help myself. "He's pretty much the worst referee in history."

Sheridan laughed, only slightly drunk. "I'll bet he turns it into a three-man fight before round two."

"Come on, Sheridan," I said as the boxers circled each other. "Whoever heard of a referee fighting?"

The first two rounds were pretty stereotypical. Appleton and the other guy, Varley, fought equally, Whistler only having to break them up a couple times. During round three, Varley, like a super-heavyweight, knocked Appleton down.

"One, two..." Whistler halfheartedly counted into the megaphone. Varley came up behind him and whispered something while glancing at the crowd, stopping him before he could get to "three."

As Appleton got to his feet, Whistler clenched his hand and slammed the megaphone onto the canvas. He pummeled Varley. Jaw, jaw, gut, side, nose. Varley stumbled backward before belting Whistler, who recovered quickly and took him in a headlock.

Appleton stood bewildered for a moment, but then apparently, decided to join forces against the lesser of two evils. He yanked Whistler off Varley and threw him into a corner, then proceeded to pound his face. Whistler kneed him below the belt and tackled him to the canvas, pinning his chest with his knees and throwing hooks at his jaws.

When Varley came up behind him, he rolled off Appleton, kicked to his feet and landed an uppercut right under the jaw.

"What'd I tell ya?" Sheridan confirmed.

He watched until Appleton pinned Whistler's arms behind his back, giving Varley unlimited punching access, and then climbed into the ring. Whistler had taken at least a dozen punches in the gut before Sheridan pulled Varley off him.

Whistler proceeded to elbow Appleton in the gut and then charge

Varley again, pummeling him as Sheridan restrained him. Cliff watched a few seconds before muttering something under his breath and jumping into the ring to help Sheridan out, which only caused a bigger mess.

Before I knew it, the ring was a fishbowl of five brawling sharks, scrambling across the floor and falling into the ropes, punching and body slamming. Too many illegal moves to count.

Afraid someone would end up in the hospital, I glanced at the amused men around me, who looked as if they had no intentions of breaking up the most entertainment they'd probably ever had.

Rolling my eyes, I grabbed a rope and crossed the ring to get to the bell, dodging the brawling guys. When that didn't work, I yelled into the megaphone. And when that didn't work, I found Sheridan and managed to yank him aside.

"Testosterone fails at breaking up testosterone," I spat. "Get Cliff out of the ring."

"You sure?"

"Get Cliff!" I repeated, my voice louder, though no one else could hear me above the racket.

Sheridan shrugged and then yanked Cliff away from Appleton and Varley. I could practically feel Cliff's eyes widening when he saw me in the ring, but I continued with my plan.

When Appleton ducked to avoid a punch from Whistler, I landed a kick to his jaw to make him stumble backward, then landed another as hard as I could below the belt. He doubled over and winced, leaving me with only Varley, who I got in the side before repeating my below-the-belt move.

Whistler wanted to go after him as he fell, but I grabbed Whistler's wrist and pulled him to the other side of the ring, then placed my palm on his chest in a no-more gesture. His gaze held mine.

Once I was sure he was calm, I took the megaphone, addressing the five bruised brawlers, then the general audience. "We'll take a brief recess before the next fight. It's safe to say that both fighters in this round are disqualified." The crowd gaped at me, and then, as I replaced the megaphone, burst into applause.

I shrugged, glancing at Whistler, whose puffy, bloody face was very different than it had been a few minutes ago. He smiled a slanted smile at me, then clapped along with the crowd.

Sheridan stepped back into the ring and spoke to Whistler. "Maybe I should take it from here." Though he was covered in bruises too, maybe even a little blood, he sounded sober enough. Now I believed he'd do a better job completely wasted than Whistler.

I climbed down from the ring, into the cheering audience, and headed to Cliff. "Anything broken?" I asked, giving him a onceover. He didn't look too badly hurt, probably since he'd been the last to jump into the fight.

"No," he muttered. "What about you?"

"Nope. Don't know about the other guys, though." I bit my lip, glancing at the ring. Sheridan was announcing the next round, but Whistler was gone.

"Maybe we should go," I said reluctantly, the extra murmurs and stares making me feel self-conscious now that I'd broadcasted my presence. "I don't think things can get more entertaining than that."

* * * *

After I'd turned my light out and Tut had crawled onto my bed, I was still nowhere near ready for sleep. I hadn't even been able to bear swapping my clothes for pajamas. The faint lingering scent of smoky, beer-filled Man Cave was bizarrely comforting to me.

Tap tap tap. I shot up at the strange, quick sound. "What the heck?" *Tap tap tap.*

After gently moving Tut aside, I climbed out of bed and then peeled back my curtains. The glass framed a familiar silhouette. More shocked at how thrilled I was than at the fact that he was there in the first place, I lifted the pane and did my best to whisper.

"You followed me? How did you know which room was mine?"

He smiled a slanted smile. "Shadows reveal a lot."

A knocking on my door made me jump. "Selk, I'm going to bed," Mom called. "Have breakfast with me in the morning?"

I winced, willing myself not to stutter. "Um... Yeah, Mom. Goodnight."

"Goodnight."

I counted to five before daring to speak again. "I live with... Um... My mom lives with me. She never met anyone after Dad left. I don't want her to be alone." I stopped myself from further explanation, though most of it was true. Defensiveness about living with your parents sounded way seventeen-year-old.

"That's sweet," he said, to my relief. "I miss my parents. My foster parents. Whatever they were." I thought I saw a little blush. "Um... Well... You're probably wondering why I'm hanging off the side of your house like a stalker. I just wanted to see if you wanted to go somewhere or hang out or something."

I grinned. "Where should we go?"

He shrugged. "We'll know when we get there. Come on."

Luckily, there was a little "pre-roof" just below the second story. Still, Whistler would have at least had to find a box or something to stand on so he could pull himself onto it. Unless he was just in incredible shape from training.

After I grabbed my coat, he took my hand and stepped aside so I could climb out the window. *He took my hand.* The butterflies glided around as if I'd just met a celebrity or something, and I'd only been star-struck once or twice in my life.

When I just stood there staring at him, he threw me a questioning glance.

I shook my head, mostly at myself, and blurted, "You know what? I like you, Whistler Casebolt."

He smiled that dry smile, one that grew on me. "One out of, what, a couple thousand people in this small town? Not bad."

We climbed down and then jogged to the sidewalk, keeping the pace until my house had disappeared from sight.

The streets weren't empty, due to it being Friday night, but I wasn't afraid of anyone recognizing me and reporting back to Mom or Cliff. Darkness came in handy sometimes.

"So, we still don't know where we're going?" I asked as we walked on, passing the familiar art shops, then Mack's, then the gym.

"Nope."

"Well, let's just be nomads and wander around aimlessly then."

We walked a few more moments before he said, "I was curious about the Egyptian-Croatian girl with the merciless punches, so I called the *Riverwood Chronicle*. They've never heard of you."

Swallowing hard, I forced my eyes not to widen and my mind to work fast. "Most of them wouldn't have. I'm new. The boxing thing was only my second assignment."

"What was your first?"

"Um..." My confidence was fleeing. "Egyptian things. They're...very open to suggestions from their staff. It's a pleasant rarity."

He glanced at me, then, to my relief, dropped the subject. "Sometimes, I wish I would have gone to college for something normal like reporting. Once a bizarre life, always a bizarre life, right?"

I shrugged. "Not necessarily. If bizarre is what you want, then yeah, but I say true passion wins over what you think *should* be done."

He threw me a half smile that I thought held a pinch of doubt. "And reporting is your true passion?"

"Y...yes," I said, aware that I was sealing myself into the lie like a mummy in a tomb. "I mean, you can have more than one passion. Like my boxing hobby." I threw a light jab to his jaw, but immediately regretted touching him. The butterflies hatched relentlessly.

He jabbed me back, though it felt as if his fingers brushed my cheek. For the first time, I seriously wanted to kiss a guy, one I barely knew. And I didn't know how to handle that.

"Thanks for bailing me out at Man Cave," he said after a few seconds. "That was kind of awesome."

I was about to respond when we had to stop in front of a bed-and-breakfast for a man to get out of a taxicab. Something about him was strange. His features were dark, unfamiliar, and yet, at the same time, they reminded me of someone.

I squinted to see if I could recognize him, but that did little good. What nationality was he? Indian? Italian?

As he thanked and paid the taxi driver, I realized he was neither. His accent was Arabic.

"What is it, Selk?" Whistler asked.

"I think he's Egyptian," I whispered. "It's just weird, is all, seeing another Egyptian in Snow Hill."

I must have whispered louder than I'd thought, because, as the taxi drove off, the man stopped on the bottom step of the bed-and-breakfast and faced Whistler and me. He squinted as I'd done a few seconds ago.

Clearing my throat, I tried to ignore him and continue down the sidewalk, but he blocked my path. He was middle-aged with black eyes above a blunt, arched nose and thin beard.

When Whistler came up beside me, the man studied him before turning his attention to me. "Selk?"

My eyes widened. "How—"

I started at an abrupt flash beside me, followed by another and another. Silhouettes of light bounced off Whistler's skin and disappeared. Once they stopped, he stumbled backward as if breaking free from paralysis, shaking his head.

"What the—"

The man clapped his hands in joy and spoke, cutting me off. "I can't believe it. Both of you, in one place! Come with me."

I backed away, beyond freaked out. Where had that light come from?

He grabbed Whistler's wrist and pulled him toward the door of the bed-and-breakfast. Whistler punched his nose and shook himself free before taking my hand and bolting down the sidewalk.

"Wait!" the man called, his voice muffled by the blow. "Let me explain!"

"I don't want him to explain," Whistler muttered. We ran several blocks until we reached the edge of the park. Even he had to catch his breath this time.

"What just happened?" I asked after a few seconds.

"I don't know," he said. "I'm kind of scared too."

"Do you know that man?"

"No," he said. "It seemed as if he knew *you*. You've never seen him before?"

I shook my head, and he sighed and ran his fingers through his hair, then walked to the edge of the pond to glimpse his reflection.

"He didn't even seem to notice my bruises, but he knew..." He stopped himself, facing me. "Look, I'm sorry. I just wanted to hang out. I had no idea something so weird would happen."

I joined him by the pond. "So you do have an idea of what that light was." When he didn't say anything, I pressed, "I've noticed quite a few strange things about you since we've met. Nothing I can remember in detail, just little comments and observations. Was that just a flashlight or was it something..." I searched for the right word, "paranormal?"

He hesitated. "I like you too, Selk. Which is why I don't know if I should answer that."

I nodded, though his confirmation of the truth didn't mean I wasn't shocked. "Paranormal it is then." His other confirmation, the one about him liking me, would have to make a later playdate with my butterflies. "How paranormal are you talking?"

"You're not surprised?"

"I'm astonished." I paced in the snow. "I've always believed in something more than what we can see."

He laughed, harder than I'd ever seen him laugh. "If you only knew how relevant and ironic that statement was." Stepping closer, he brushed a strand of hair out of my eyes, and I dared to lift my fingers to his bruised face.

"How long before your face heals?" I whispered.

"Not long."

My nerves getting the better of me, I pulled away and turned my back to the bridge. "It's getting colder. Maybe I should head back."

As if expecting me to say that, he didn't protest, just said, "I'll walk you, but let's sidestep the bed-and-breakfast, okay?"

CHAPTER FOUR

Only Minutes

"Selk?" My head snapped up at the mentioning of my name. "Selk," Brandie, my honey-blonde friend, repeated, "you've been acting weird lately."

"Wanna talk about it?" Tall-and-slender Lynette, my other friend, added.

I sighed, shutting my locker. "Not really." I hadn't seen anyone, except for Mom, the rest of the weekend. Maybe Whistler was avoiding me. Maybe I was avoiding him.

Brandie stepped in front of me. "It's a guy." At my wide eyes, she nodded at Lynette. "Yep. *Finally*. How can we help?"

I stepped around her. "Not even a question? Just an accusation?"

"A true accusation." Her face fell. "Wait, it's not Cliff, is it? Tell me you didn't finally wise up and see how gorgeous he is."

I laughed at her, then at Lynette, who mirrored Brandie's expression. "Cliff is like my big brother. We won't happen in a million years. He's all yours."

I laughed again at Brandie's audible sigh of relief. "There *is* a guy," she pressed, "and if you don't tell, I'll find out." When I didn't say anything, she added, "Okay, I'll settle for you admitting that you have a crush."

I was taken aback by the word. *Crush?* Had I ever used that word before when it didn't involve kicking in someone's skull?

"Y…yeah. I have a crush." My hands trembled. "I *actually* have a crush."

Lynette, usually the quieter of the two, startled me when she squealed right along with Brandie. "Who is he?" Lynette prodded. "Is it James from homeroom? I'll bet it's James."

I shook my head. "He doesn't go to school here. He's a little older."

"And you're *positive* it's not Cliff?" Brandie pressed.

"Positive," I confirmed, realizing we'd somehow made it to the front doors of the school.

I didn't say anything else as we walked down the steps, just blocked out the relentless questions of the two reporters at my sides. As we reached the bottom step, I stopped so fast they bumped into me. I hadn't expected a pair of eyes to be watching me, waiting for me after school.

A pair of green eyes. A sulking figure wearing black and blue clothes, not bruises, leaning against a lamppost.

My breath catching, I glided to him in a daze, leaving Brandie and Lynette by the steps. How had he found out?

"Guess I'm not the only one who's good at keeping secrets," he said, his voice and face cold.

Lowering my eyes, I traced a pattern with my sneaker in the thin layer of snow on the sidewalk. "How did you find out? Cliff?"

"Sheridan. He kind of blurted it, just a bit drunkenly."

I sighed, unable to blame Sheridan, even though I wanted to. I deserved full credit for this lie. "Boxing is my senior project, not an article for a magazine. I'd make a lousy reporter."

"How old are you?" he asked, ignoring my remarks.

Forcing myself to meet his eyes, I admitted, "Seventeen. For a couple months, anyway." Turning his back, he muttered something under his breath. "Two months, Whistler," I repeated. "What's the big deal? You don't want to hang out with a baby? Cliff is twenty-five. Plus, however reluctantly, I hang out with Sheridan, and he's got a couple years on Cliff."

He whirled, facing me again. "I knew there was a catch. You were too perfect."

I scoffed. "I'm nowhere near perfect. I'm just as screwed up as you think you are." Taking a hesitant step closer, I added, "I'm not rejecting you for hiding things from me, because I understand. So please don't reject my decisions."

He sighed, shaking his head so his black hoodie fell down. "I keep forgetting your age."

"*My* age? How mature is climbing up to windows in the middle of the night for an extemporaneous stroll through town?"

"Romeo did it," he muttered.

"Romeo was *my* age. And not real."

"Selk, when I said I liked you, I meant it."

"So did I."

"I don't think you understand. I..." He trailed off, grabbing the lamppost and rocking on his heels. "It doesn't matter, anyway."

"Yes, it does," I blurted, grabbing his arm and spinning him around. "I've never met anyone like you. You're special."

"You don't even know me."

"You don't have to know a person to trust them."

His eyes softened, and he leaned closer. Muttering something unintelligible, he grabbed my hand and led me down the sidewalk, an alley and then a narrower abandoned alley with a dead end.

"What—"

His lips were on mine before I realized he'd cut me off. Recovering from the shock, I kissed him back and ran my fingers through his hair, unable to comprehend the enormity of the magic feeling that had nothing to do with his paranormal secret.

Unable to get close enough, I wrapped my arms around his waist and kissed him deeper. He backed me, backpack and all, against an old door and closed every fragment of space between us, his mouth fiercely working mine. My blood shook from the hectic moment, but I'd never been one to back away from adrenaline. His shoulders, chest, face, I'd never met a guy so completely attractive, as irresistible as birds found the sky.

I'd never met a guy who so completely understood me.

I was still kissing him even as he pulled away.

"Before we attempt this, I need to know one thing."

"What?" I breathed.

"Do you honestly want to be with me?"

All self-restraint gone, I tackled him, kissing him so hard he stumbled backward. "Does that answer your question?" I asked before briefly attacking him again. "You're pretty dreamy, Whistler Casebolt, but don't go getting an inflated ego."

He smiled, not so dryly this time. "I guess even a pathetic jerk can win the lottery."

I traced his lips with my fingers, murmuring, "They're the jerks, remember?"

He kissed me for another minute or two and then we left.

* * * *

The moment I walked into my house, all thoughts of Whistler vanished. Whose voice was that, in the kitchen, talking to Mom?

Tut greeted me at the door, and I petted him before creeping up to the kitchen, the muffled conversation growing clearer with each step I took.

"Of course you're here now, since she's suddenly useful!" I'd never heard Mom so angry before.

"She has no choice. None of us do." My breath caught. I recognized his accent before I saw his face. The Egyptian man from Friday night. He knew Mom? "If only I was at risk, I wouldn't have come back. It's my whole family, including Selk."

Family? What was he talking about?

"If she doesn't return to Egypt with me," he continued, "at any moment, we could die, fall dead in a blink of an eye. Do you want to see her die, see doctors baffled by an autopsy report of a healthy young girl?"

I couldn't see Mom from this angle—I was hiding behind the table in the entryway—but I heard her voice choke.

After a long silent moment, she said, so softly I had to strain my ears, "What you're asking her to do... Isn't that a risk as well? You nearly died yourself doing the same thing."

"I came out, and I went alone," the man protested. "She won't be alone. He'll be with her."

"I still don't know who you're talking about. The only boy she ever spends time with is her boxing instructor, Cliff, who's like family, and she came home early Friday night. And his hair isn't even dark blond like you said. It's black."

"He was like a boxing instructor," he muttered. "He gave me this."

Only when he pointed to his face did I see the yellowish-green bruise by his nose, obviously a couple days old. My stomach twisted. Whistler had punched a long-lost uncle of mine or something, and that uncle had blabbed to Mom that I'd snuck out of the house. With a boy she didn't know.

I'd planned on interrupting their conversation, but I couldn't. Not yet. Instead, I kept listening.

"Cvijeta, I know you remember the things you saw in Egypt, how real the magic is."

Mom went to Egypt? Maybe I should have known, but I'd always assumed she'd met Dad in the States.

"Which is why I hoped to keep Selk from them."

The man laughed. "You said she's embraced her Egyptian heritage. I wouldn't be lying if I said it makes me happy that she wants to study Egyptology."

"I'm beginning to wish she would have turned her boxing hobby into a career instead. It'd be less dangerous."

The man rubbed his face. "More painful." He paused, then said, "You really don't know the other young man she was with on Friday?"

"No. I can't believe she'd sneak out of the house for any boy. She's never even shown interest in dating."

"Young girls grow up," the man said matter-of-factly. "Nonetheless, he will be the one to accompany her. Though I can't emphasize enough how astonished I was to find him here with her. I expected months, maybe years, of searching." He laughed again. "Not to mention, even though to American parents, he was born in Croatia! What a coincidence that *Ummi* and *Abbi* picked a child with ties to Croatia to gain time for us."

I clamped a hand over my mouth to keep from gasping. I'd picked up a few Arabic words and phrases while studying Egyptology websites and books. This man's parents had been Whistler's foster parents.

"I still don't agree with that," Mom spat. "It was a cruel thing to use an innocent child to—"

"The boy was unwanted," the man interrupted. "What kind of a life could he have had? I believe he was fated to help us. How likely was it for him to move here, not to mention, grow close to Selk?"

"I don't like that either. I don't know anything about this boy, except that he's been on his own since he was a young teen. He must be a rebel by now with no guardian to guide him."

I stood and walked into the kitchen right when the man said, "Regardless, he seems to care about our daughter." They turned toward my gasp.

"You're my *father?*" I asked, my voice hoarse.

His eyes widened, but he smiled. "Yes, dear Selk. You're my daughter. And what a proud father I am to see the strong, beautiful young woman you've become."

He opened his arms for a hug, but I stepped back, my defenses stronger than when in a sparring session.

"What's all this talk about death? Why am I in danger of dying? Why is *Whistler* in danger?"

"So that's the boy's name," Mom said, though the man—my father—didn't look surprised. "Selk, why have you been sneaking around? You know you can talk to me about anything. Is this boy trouble? Is that why you didn't want me—"

"Why did *you* sneak around, Mom? You knew where my dad was the whole time, didn't you?" I turned to my so-called father. "Answer me. How are Whistler and I in danger?"

"Selk," he said calmly, "everything will be fine once you and Whistler go to Egypt with me and do what must be done." Tut walked into the kitchen, weaving around first my legs and then my dad's. "I'm glad to see you liked your birthday gift well enough to keep."

"Birthday gift?" I looked at Tut, then to the face of the man who claimed he was my dad. I remembered my grandpa, who'd been more like my father. He'd known.

Hurt. Betrayal. It was too much.

"The heck I'm going to Egypt with you!"

Mom and my supposed dad called me as I bolted back into the snow, but I ignored them, tears blurring my vision. How could this have been the best day of my life only minutes before I'd walked into my house?

Usually, it was Cliff who held the punching bag when I was upset as I tortured it and vented until I felt better. I surprised myself by wanting to go to someone else for comfort this time. He and I were involved in something dangerous, so I needed to warn him.

Hopefully, he was where I assumed.

Cliff was saying goodbye to a student as I walked to the boxing corner of the gym, and Sheridan was sparring with Bateson in the ring.

31

I forced a smile as Cliff walked over. "You're just in time. Your boyfriend's here." He glanced at Bateson with a grin that should have made me punch him. When I didn't, he frowned. "You all right?"

Of course I couldn't hide it. I rarely got this upset. "Yeah," I said, doing my best to keep him from asking questions. "Have you seen Whistler?"

He narrowed his eyes. "Did the scum hurt you?"

I shook my head. "No. I just need to double-check a question I asked him during the interview."

Cliff hesitated, as if he still didn't buy my explanation, but eventually gave in. "He's around here somewhere. I saw him carry his gear to the locker room a few minutes ago to change."

I nodded and averted my eyes, the tears trying to well up again. "Great. I'll wait."

At least I didn't have to track him down at his and Sheridan's apartment. I'd never been there, but I knew it was past the park. The sooner I saw him, the better.

"Are you going to keep pretending like I don't know you're lying, or are you going to tell me what's wrong?"

I tried to sigh in exasperation at Cliff's perseverance, but it came out shaky. "I'm fine," I said, my voice just as wavering. "Just one complicated bad thing to ruin an otherwise great day."

"Since when have you cried over something small?" When I sniffled out of reflex, he lifted my chin so I'd look at him. "What happened, Selk?"

The tears fell hard, so I walked behind the punching bag to hide from Sheridan and Bateson and everyone else. I could imagine how worried Cliff got when I rested my forehead against the punching bag instead of swinging at it. I broke down, just a little, but enough to startle even me. The last time I'd broken down had been when my grandpa had died.

"Selk, what's wrong?" Cliff repeated, wrapping an arm around my shoulders.

I just sobbed quietly, unable to bring myself to look at him. "Almost everything," I whispered, my voice choked with tears.

"Well, tell me and maybe I can help," Cliff murmured, his strong arm squeezing my shoulder. "You want to sit down and talk about it?"

I was about to say yes when Whistler walked up, wearing nothing but his boxing shorts and boxing shoes, his gloves in his hand.

"Selk? What happened?" He glanced questioningly at Cliff, who offered no comment.

Not caring how stupid and melodramatic I looked, I broke away from a startled Cliff and threw my arms around Whistler's smooth torso, giving the tears full control.

After dropping his gloves, he wrapped his arms around me, and I quietly sobbed against his skin. I tried to tell him what I'd just heard, but I couldn't get it past the tears.

"Selk?" he repeated, his voice soft.

Wiping my eyes, I pulled back slightly to whisper, "The man we saw Friday night…" So Cliff could hear the next part, I pulled away completely and said, still sniffling, "My dad just showed up out of nowhere." I didn't know if Cliff was more bewildered over my running into Whistler's arms or what I'd just said.

"What?" Cliff and Whistler remarked in unison.

"And my mom and grandpa knew where he was the whole time."

"Where?" Cliff asked, stepping closer.

"I don't know," I said, taking a deep breath to stop the tears once and for all. "I just know they kept in contact with him. And now…" I looked back to Whistler. "Can I talk to you alone for a second?"

"Of course," he said, glancing warily at Cliff.

Cliff looked shocked, maybe even hurt, which made me feel bad. He knew more about my life than anyone, even my mom, but this was something I couldn't tell him. Something, for once, he wouldn't understand.

His jaw taut, he nodded. "I'll just…um…pummel this some more."

I threw him a look I hoped said, *Sorry.* He turned his attention to the canvas bag and said nothing else, beating it hard.

Whistler led me to a lonely weight bench in the opposite corner, far away from Cliff and far enough from the few people on treadmills and exercise bikes. We sat on the long, leathery seat, and after gathering my thoughts, I said, "He knows everything about you. I eavesdropped on him telling my mom about seeing us on Friday before I interrupted their conversation."

Whistler furrowed his brows, surprised I'd started off with him as the topic. "How——"

"*Ummi* and *Abbi*," I said. "He called your foster parents Mother and Father in Arabic." I lowered my eyes, not sure how to tell him. "My dad's parents, my *grandparents*, were your foster parents. And I think they used you."

"Used me? What do you mean?"

If I didn't fully understand it myself, I had no clue how to explain everything to Whistler, especially with pieces still missing, but I had to try.

"I overheard so much, I really don't know where to start," I said. "The most urgent thing is, somehow, for some reason, you're in danger, at the least, and I could die at any moment."

I repeated every detail I remembered from the conversation between my mom and—it still didn't feel real—dad. I fell into a mentally drained silence, and Whistler appeared to fall into a contemplative one.

After a moment, he said, "And you don't trust him?"

"How can I? He's been gone my whole life and only shows up when he needs me to do something potentially fatal. I can't even trust my mom. I can't even trust my late grandpa." I could see where I got my lying habit from now. I'd been born with it.

Whistler ran his fingers through his hair, shaking his head and muttering, "This is insane." He paused, then said, "It looks like we only have two options—run or confront your father."

I rested my head on my hands. "I don't know if I can do that."

"We may not have a choice," he said gently. "Especially if he said you'll die if you don't do whatever it is you have to do."

I shook my head, then pleadingly looked at Whistler. "Will you tell me what you're keeping from me now? My dad mentioned, however impossible, magic. Between us, maybe we can put the pieces together."

Whistler nodded. "Yeah. You definitely need to know this now. If your dad really is my foster parents' son, he wasn't lying about the magic." Averting his eyes, he continued, "Remember how I told you about my foster parents kicking me out when they found me going through their stuff? Well, there was more to it than that."

"Yeah, you said you had a bit of amnesia."

"Not exactly amnesia," he said. "I can remember random moments of my time with them. They're just foggy. My memories after I left are clearer, after I got mixed up with that stupid amulet."

My eyes widened. "Amulet?"

"Yeah," he said. "The Eye of Horus, an authentic artifact in my foster parents' collection. They did contact me once, a couple weeks after I'd left, but it was only to accuse me of stealing the amulet. I told them I had no use for anything of theirs. Don't know if they ever found it or not, and I don't care." When I didn't say anything, just bit my lip, he looked at me, and asked, "What? Did your dad mention the amulet?"

"No," I said. "I don't know if it's coincidence or not, but there have been articles broadcasting the mysterious theft of an Eye of Horus amulet from The British Museum in London. I know there are tons of those artifacts, but what are the odds…"

"That it could be the same one," he finished, laughing in disbelief. "After everything that's happened to me, I could believe anything. Whoever stole the amulet from my foster parents could have sold it to the museum. If that's the same one, then we're definitely talking magic."

I expectantly searched his eyes. "What kind of magic?"

After glancing around to make sure no one had approached, he looked at me, and whispered, "Watch my forehead." He pushed his boy-bangs aside and closed his eyes, revealing nothing but smooth, pale skin.

The skin quivered, twisted. Though it happened instantly, it felt like slow motion. An oval shape formed and stretched, a corner at either side, framed by little sandy needles, then peeled, revealing a background of white. The last thing to pop up was a dark spot in the center enclosed by a thick neon-blue ring.

The eye blinked once before disappearing.

Whistler opened his green eyes and let his hair fall back into place, whispering, "The only thing I know is that after the incident with the amulet, some weird light show happened and then I turned into a Cyclops."

Fully expecting him to say psychic powers or seeing dead people or something the world had kind of gotten used to, I was speechless when he'd said the word. I didn't know if it was considered a power or if it was what he was.

"Ever since," he continued, "I've been able to see through doors, walls, pretty much anything. I thought it was cool at first, but it got old after a while."

I stared at him—as if he had a third eye—but I didn't know how much more I could handle. Averting my eyes, I breathed, "I certainly didn't expect that."

"You're probably more confused now."

I nodded. "Yeah. Incredibly confused."

"This is a selfish question compared to everything going on, but…" He tilted my chin so I'd look at him. "Do you still want to be with me?"

I held his gaze, his rich green eyes, for a long time. I took his hand on the bench, and whispered, "Yes."

He smiled, squeezing mine. "Good."

I laughed dryly. "Do you still want to be with me, the girl with a long-lost dysfunctional family showing up out of nowhere with promises of death?"

"Yes," he said surely.

When he offered nothing more, I couldn't help but press, "Why?"

"Because you're the girl of my dreams." He kept my gaze for a moment, then pulled me closer, into his arms.

Nothing was better—everything was actually about ten times more screwed up now—but somehow, he'd made me *feel* better.

Pulling back slightly, he said, "I think you know what we have to do."

Nodding, I said, "Let's go."

I waited on the bench across from the front desk for Whistler to change back into his regular clothes. Busy forcing my mind to take a break and stop thinking, I didn't hear Cliff approach and was startled when he sat beside me.

"Selk," he said, his hushed tone serious, "what's going on? You're really scaring me."

"Cliff," I said, sighing, "I wish I could tell you. Maybe I can eventually. It's just hard for even Whistler and me to understand right now." I bit my tongue, knowing he wouldn't like the mentioning of Whistler.

Clenching his jaw, he said with a growl, "Selk, you've known the guy just over a week. How could you have secrets with him? How could you shut *me* out and turn to a guy you barely know?" Narrowing his eyes, he added, "So I was wrong. It's not Bateson, after all."

"Nothing is going on between Whistler and me," I lied. Before Cliff could comment, Whistler walked to the door, glancing at me.

"I'll see you later," I muttered to Cliff, then followed Whistler outside.

Once we'd passed a few shops, I said, "I'm sorry. Cliff's suspicious about us now. I should have been able to control my emotions."

"Why, because you're a robot?" He grabbed my hand and squeezed it. "It's all right. It was a bad idea to keep this from everyone. Especially people who know us."

"Well, we don't have to broadcast it," I said, holding his hand for a second before letting it go. "We'll figure that out later."

CHAPTER FIVE

Falling Dead

Whistler and I found Mom and my father standing by the bookcase in the living room. They looked up at our approach.

"I'm so glad you came back, Selk," my father said, "and that you brought Whistler with you."

"Only because I apparently have no choice," I spat.

Mom took a step toward us, her face unreadable as she appraised Whistler. "How old are you?"

I sighed. Of course Mom was more concerned about my relationship status than my impending death.

"Twenty-one," he said without any drama.

"Cliff's four years older than him, Mom," I said before we could get into an interrogation about Whistler and me. "I've always assumed I'm allowed to have older friends."

"Cliff is different," Mom protested.

"Cvijeta," my dad said, placing a hand on her shoulder, "the boy brings no trouble as far as I can tell." He pointed to his face. "He stood up for Selk when he thought I was a threat."

Well, wasn't that ironic. The only person who didn't hate Whistler was the one *I* hated right now. Refusing to acknowledge any common ground with my father, I said, "Well, you came all this way to find us, and we're here, so start talking. Why are we in danger, and what do you want us to do?"

"Not what I want," he said, "but what you *must* do. Yes, you'll die, Selk, if you don't do this, and Whistler will too."

My eyes widened. I exchanged glances with Whistler. "You said he was in danger. You didn't say he would die for sure."

"If you and Whistler are successful in Egypt, none of us will die, but we have to act fast. I don't want to worry either of you, but you, him, myself and even my parents could fall dead at any moment, no symptoms, no warning."

My dad replaced a book he'd been looking at on the shelf and then selected another. "We need to leave for Egypt as soon as possible. Tomorrow morning was the earliest flight I was able to book on such short notice, even with connections. I spent all weekend making the arrangements after running into you two. Without connections, it could have taken weeks or months, especially since it's winter, when the climate is nicest."

"Egypt, *tomorrow*?" I repeated. "I don't even have a passport."

"You and Whistler both have passports now," my dad said, then gestured for us to sit. "You need to be informed before we go. The task at hand isn't easy."

When we hesitated, he sat in the middle of the couch and gestured again for us to sit on either side of him. Whistler glanced at me, then sat on his right. I sat on his left. Mom quietly excused herself to the kitchen.

"First, Selk," my dad said, opening the book, which was one of my Egyptian history books, "do you know for whom you were named?"

I shrugged. "My Grandma Veronika on Mom's side, who I never met. Selket is just linked to Isis in Egyptian mythology. I wouldn't call that being named after someone."

"You're only partly right."

When he offered nothing else, just scanned a couple pages for something, I countered sarcastically, "Was I named after you?"

He smiled and shook his head, still searching the book. "My name is Zahid Yahya Baioumi."

"Zahid, then," I muttered. "I certainly can't call you 'Dad.'"

"I understand," he said, a hint of sadness tracing his voice. "Even if you reject me, you need to understand the history of our family, beginning with Selket, the scorpion guardian you were named for."

He settled on a page with an ancient illustration of a female Egyptian with a giant scorpion on her head, then continued. "Selket wasn't part of Isis, but was adapted to that over time in Egyptian culture. She was a protector and healer, curing scorpion stings and serpent bites and protecting those already dead. She was favored by kings for this."

Some of this sounded familiar, but I'd never studied Selket in detail.

Tutankhamen, Ramses and other mummies of the like seemed to always be the stars of the show for aspiring Egyptologists, not myths.

"So I was named after an Egyptian goddess," I said. "Why is that a big deal?"

"It is a big deal," Zahid said, "because you, my parents and I are, as far as I know, her only living descendants."

I stood, scoffing. "You come here out of nowhere announcing you're my dad, then expect me to believe in Egyptian gods and goddesses? Even if Selket or any of the other mythological figures were real, how could you possibly trace an ancestry that far back? That's like…ancient."

"We have our ways," my dad said. "And I'm not expecting you to believe in myths. The figures of Egyptian mythology were just ordinary people with gifts." When I didn't say anything, just crossed my arms and clenched my jaw, he added, pointing at Whistler, "You can't tell me you find this so hard to believe. You saw the glow the other night. And I'm sure he showed you his own power."

My eyes softened, the reminder sobering. "You know that Whistler's a—"

"Cyclops, as you would say?" He laughed a little. "Yes, I know. He was given power by the Eye of Horus amulet *Ummi*, *Abbi* and I spent years searching for. They finally found it in America when Whistler was fourteen, where they purchased it from a traveling archaeologist. They made sure Whistler would find it and absorb some of its power. He apparently absorbed a lot, because we're still alive." I was about to comment, but he held up a hand to stop me. "This must be confusing. Let me explain. Many artifacts the 'gods' and 'goddesses' of ancient Egypt guarded or were associated with were infused with their power. Since then, for millennia, their descendants have ensured the safekeeping of these in their rightful resting places, where their powers lie dormant and benign.

"We can sense them, the 'active' artifacts, and can't rest until all have been stilled. We're drawn to them. Some even glow in our presence."

He and I both glanced at Whistler, who listened intently. Maybe, aside from Whistler's good looks and personality, that was why I'd been drawn to him—I'd, however subtly, sensed the amulet's power.

"After practice, we just know. We know how many have been

removed from their resting places and how many have been awakened. As descendants of Selket, this amulet is the last object to have been disturbed, our last responsibility."

I was starting to understand—a little—but something big didn't make sense. "How can that be the last one? There are countless artifacts, a lot of which are spread out in museums around the world. How could a few people make sure all of them are accounted for? And even if we do return the amulet, what's to stop someone from moving it again?" My eyes widened. With everything that had happened, I only now remembered a huge problem. "It's the amulet in the articles, isn't it?" When Zahid nodded, I said, exasperated, "We don't even know where it's at."

"It's in my room at the bed-and-breakfast."

I gasped. "You're the thief?" Mystery solved, after all.

"They're the thieves. The museum, archaeologists, even Egyptologists. They stole from the kings, queens, guardians of Egypt, and continue to do so. Because of that, descendants of Horus and Sakhmet and Khonsu and Isis and Selket and all the other gifted ancients suffer. So, to answer your questions, there have been many working hard over time to retrieve and deliver every single misplaced artifact. Even if someone were to move them, they would not be moving the true artifacts, as the descendants restored them to a place where non-descendants can't go—Post World, the former post of the thought-to-be god or goddess, where their power was stored.

"Once an artifact associated with or guarded by the appropriate figure is placed in that post, it will appear, should another find it in our world, in the spot parallel to where it was left in Post World. For instance, if you returned an artifact to Post World's version of a pyramid, it would duplicate and reappear in that same pyramid on Earth."

"Post World," Whistler repeated. "So, is that like an alternate Egypt or something?"

"Sort of, but in a condensed form. Mostly the artificial things that were crafted during ancient Egypt, the artifacts, of course, but also the buildings, and even the mummies. Most of what you see in the pyramids and crumbling palaces today are lively and frightening in Post World. Especially the mummies, the most important treasures of the guardians."

I tried to fight my equal terror and excitement, but both grew with every new revelation. "It really is true..." I whispered. My voice louder, I added, "This amulet is essentially the Eye of Horus. Why is it associated with Selket?"

"Because it was one of the artifacts she guarded."

My mouth opened a little. "She guarded it, like, the actual amulet?"

My dad nodded. "And you, Selk, must return it. I tried in vain to return it myself after your grandparents asked me to, but only a female can return the amulet, as Selket was female, and a descendant may only enter the portal once per artifact. My failed attempt sent the amulet into the hands of the museum. They found its earthly symbol before I could leave Post World. I worked for years to crack the museum's security code until I finally stole it back."

"Where does Whistler come in?" I asked. "Why does he have to go?"

Zahid sighed, looking at Whistler. "I'm sorry, but I understand if you don't forgive me or *Ummi* and *Abbi*, your foster parents. We can't absorb artifact power because we already possess the power of descendants, but those unaffiliated can. *Ummi* and *Abbi* chose an orphaned child at random to raise, but I guess your link to Croatia stood out to them because of Selk and Cvijeta.

"We needed the amulet's power to be lessened, spread out, so they emptied some of it into you by letting you stumble upon it. With the power separated, there was less immediacy of us, of Selk," he glanced at me, "falling dead—the punishment for not fulfilling our duties. That meant you would die too, should we be unable to return the artifact to Post World, but we had more time to succeed."

"Now we have no clue how much time, if any, we have to retrieve the artifact, right?" I asked, my heart pounding with the urgency of the situation. My father nodded. "What about Whistler?" I added. "Will emptying his power or whatever hurt him? *Kill* him?"

"No," Zahid reassured. "It'll free him and all of us, so he must enter the portal to Post World with you. Your grandmother returned many artifacts in her day, but now she's too old and fragile. Post World is a relentless place, requiring physical endurance and strength. Despite her knowledge of how it works, she wouldn't have a chance." He paused, searching my face. "I left to save your life, Selk, to keep you from the fear of death peeking over your shoulder. I promised your mother I'd come back when the last artifact had been retrieved and safely stored, but I had no idea it would take so long. Please know I wouldn't have left, wouldn't be asking you to do this, if it weren't a matter of your life and death."

I walked back to the couch and sat, averting my eyes in thought. My first kiss. My dad's return. My magical duty. Threats of death. All in one day.

"If only we had more time," I said, then looked at Zahid. "What if we die before we even get to the airport?" I heard a quiet choking noise coming from the kitchen, then an Egyptian-Mau chirp. Mom was crying, and Tut must have been comforting her. There was a louder sob, then footsteps and then the front door opened and closed.

Zahid glanced toward the sound and sighed. "We can't think about that, but yes, it would help tremendously if we could find another person or two to temporarily share the burden." He apologetically looked at Whistler, who shook his head.

"If getting a third eye meant keeping Selk alive," he said, "then I don't hold any grudges."

I looked at him, touched. He really did care about me. And what scared me was that I cared about him. A lot.

"You don't think we'll be successful?" I asked Zahid.

"It's impossible to predict," he said. "Anything could happen. Flights could be cancelled, Egyptian transportation could be difficult to arrange. And surviving Post World itself is the ultimate challenge."

"You did it," I accused. "So did your mother when she was younger."

"Yes, I survived alone, but only because I'd learned the place and been there before with others," he said. "Your grandfather and I helped your grandmother, as well as your aunt. She didn't make it."

I inhaled sharply. I'd had an aunt?

The room fell quiet for a moment. I stood again, this time with determination. "I'm sure she didn't have years of self-defense and fight training like Whistler and me. You said strength and athleticism are key to surviving this mysterious world." I smiled at Whistler, my confidence growing. "If that's the case, we're certainly qualified for the job."

"She's right," he said, standing as well. "I know we can do it."

"So, what," I continued, "we have to dodge floating magic jars and punch out a few angry mummies or something?"

"Don't take this lightly," Zahid warned, unamused by my sarcasm. "Animated mummies are only part of what you'll face. And they're nothing like what you've studied about or seen in movies." Shaking his head dismissively, he said, "I'll tell you about that later. Now our primary concern is arriving in Egypt in time."

Biting my lip, I glanced at Whistler, my stomach knotted. He couldn't die. "If we did find someone else," I said, "someone strong, that wouldn't just give us more time. It'd also increase our chances of making it out of Post World alive."

Zahid frowned. "Who would we find on such short notice? Forcing and kidnapping would only draw attention from the authorities, which would hinder us, resulting in certain death. Your mother has already pleaded with me, but I refused." I was glad of that. "It's bad enough that you're caught up in this. I don't need to be worrying about her too."

"If Selk's in danger, I'll help however I can. No kidnapping necessary." We all looked up toward the voice.

Slowly, I shook my head, whispering, "No..."

Cliff.

He stepped into the living room, ignoring me. "I'm in. Just explain everything to me, and we'll be off. To Egypt, I heard?"

I jumped off the couch and leapt over to him. "Cliff," I pleaded, "you have no idea what you'd be getting yourself into. I don't even completely understand it, but I don't have a choice. You do."

"Selk," Zahid began, walking to us, "if he wants to help, why not let him? Our time would be increased, and so would your likelihood of a successful mission."

I glanced at everyone in the room, feeling helpless. Part of me wanted to do everything possible to make sure Whistler lived, but part of me wanted to keep Cliff safe.

"Selk, Cliff obviously cares a lot about you," Whistler said, standing. "And he can fight. That definitely increases the odds."

I stood quiet for a long moment, then told Zahid, "Tell Cliff everything you just told Whistler and me. Then he can decide if he still wants to go." I glanced at Cliff. "Be warned. You aren't going to believe this."

We remained standing as Zahid filled Cliff in. Once he was done, Cliff averted his eyes for a long while, then shook his head and looked at me. "Selk, I realize how big of a shock this is for you, your dad showing up out of nowhere, talking about death. I don't know what the biggest shock for *me* is—that you actually believe that fairy tale bull crap, or that someone would be heartless enough to take advantage of you when you're vulnerable."

We were talking about Zahid, but I thought I saw him glance at Whistler.

"No one is taking advantage of me," I muttered. "Believe me, I thought it was bull crap too. Then Whistler…"

I nodded at Whistler. He nodded back, then closed his eyes and pushed his boy-bangs aside. When his third eye appeared, Cliff, jaw clenched, didn't notice at first.

He did a double take.

"You're wearing green socks," Whistler said, his normal eyes still closed. "And there's a pair of gloves in your right jacket pocket."

Cliff, wide-eyed, watched Whistler hide his blue eye again, then glanced at all of us. "How… It's got to be a trick."

"Want me to describe your underwear to everyone?" Whistler threatened. "Boxer shorts, blue hearts—"

"Okay, okay. I…I believe you." Cliff ran a hand through his hair and shook his head. "I believe you, *Selk*," he corrected.

"I know the details are bizarre," I said. "Too many things add up. The amulet, Zahid's absence from my life." I threw my father a cold glance. Whistler may not have held a grudge, but I couldn't drop mine so easily. "I do trust Whistler and my own eyes. Or maybe I should say Whistler's *third* eye."

Cliff glared at Whistler. "I'll trust your runaway father before I trust him."

The remark irritated me, but I shook it aside. "Cliff, you don't have to do this."

"If I do," he said, "I'll get a third eye too. That means I can break his jaw easier—I'll be able to see past the skin and right to the bone."

"Cliff," I scolded, exasperated, "what is with you? Whistler has done nothing to you or Sheridan or really anyone else at the gym."

Cliff threw Whistler a freaked-out glare, if that was possible, then studied my face, his eyes the hardest I'd ever seen them. "Can I talk to you for a second?"

I studied him back before replying. "Yeah. Let's go to my room."

Upstairs, Cliff shut the door behind us, and we found spots to stand on my paper-and-junk-covered floor. "When's the last time you cleaned your room? Before you met me?"

"Probably." Before he could say anything else, I launched the topic. "What was that all about? I know you can't stand Whistler, but seriously. That was harsh."

He clenched his jaw. "I ran into Brandie and Lynette after you took off with him at the gym. They said you had a heated conversation with a scary-looking guy after school and then left with him."

I laughed, taken aback. "Scary-looking? They actually said that? He is *not* scary-looking. He just has messy hair. And they didn't even see his tattoo."

"They don't know he's a Cyclops, either." He paused, shaking his head as if still not believing it himself. "You do, and yet..."

I gave Cliff a challenging look. "And yet what?"

"I don't know why I didn't see it. Maybe I just chose not to. Your friends said they got you to admit that you have a crush. I just can't believe it's *him*. He's not good enough for you and he never will be."

My mouth fell open in disbelief. "Cliff, I'm appalled that you're wasting time telling me theories about my love life from Brandie and Lynette. There's a ticking clock over several people's heads, and the alarm could go off any second. My boy-crazy friends guessed tons of guys incorrectly. They even accused me of having a crush on *you*. Much to their relief, I emphasized how ridiculous that was." I was being too defensive, but even if Cliff was suspicious, I didn't need to confirm how I felt about Whistler to him. Not now. There was no time.

Probably skeptical, he averted his eyes, then looked back up at me with an unreadable expression. "There's no way you can keep me in Snow Hill now. You're not going into some haunted tomb alone with that creep."

My eyes softened, my irritation fading. "You really want to do this?"

He nodded, averting his eyes. "I miss you when you skip two days at the gym, Selk. How could I go a lifetime without seeing you?"

My throat tightening, I forced myself to stay strong. My eyes were still puffy from crying earlier. I didn't have time for another breakdown. "Cliff..." I walked to him and hugged his waist. "This means a lot."

He hugged me back, then pulled away to look at my face. "I told Sheridan I thought you were in trouble. He said to let him know and he'd help however he could. Even though he doesn't know the details, I think he might be up for coming with us."

My eyes widened. *Sheridan?* I weighed the options. Another life risked, but a greater chance. As badly as Sheridan annoyed me, he had, however few, good characteristics. And in that moment, I realized that if he died, I'd actually miss him around the gym.

Cliff put his hands on my shoulders and lowered his voice. "Selk, he'll want to go. He'll be as freaked out as I feel, but he'll want to go. He's known you for a while too and thinks of you as a little sister."

I gave him a "seriously?" look.

"He only flirts with you because it bugs me," Cliff said, reading my mind. "I think he'd miss you almost as much as I would if..."

Nodding, I reluctantly turned toward the door. "Sheridan, and that's it. Don't do anything crazy like rounding up everyone in Man Cave. There's no way Zahid can book that many last-minute seats even with connections."

I was actually thankful for Sheridan. I'd need him to help me keep Cliff and Whistler from killing each other before the mission. Maybe during.

SITES TWO–THREE: LUXOR, EGYPT, AND THE TEMPLE OF HORUS AT EDFU, EGYPT
CHAPTER SIX
Stunning Light

Never had I expected this January to include me standing in line at an airport. Especially not with the father who'd ditched Mom and me when I was a baby. Definitely not with three guys with nine eyes.

Sheridan had reacted almost the same as Cliff, only twice as badly, but he got over it eventually and agreed to help. Well, there was a brief period of freaking out after he got his third eye. Watching Cliff and Sheridan absorb power from the amulet in Zahid's bed-and-breakfast room had freaked me out. They'd been paralyzed with light like Whistler, their foreheads alternately twisting and smoothing out as the third eyes formed.

Now, after having time to let everything sink in, Sheridan took things especially well. I elbowed him whenever he'd glance at a pretty girl walking by. Cliff didn't try out his third eye because of his haircut, but Sheridan had a couple strands that fell over his forehead. Whistler, I trusted. He always looked me in *my* eyes.

"Ooh, sexy lingerie in that carryon."

I shook my head, giving up on Sheridan. I'd have been harder on him if I weren't so grateful and relieved. Four instead of two going into Post World made, according to Zahid, an incredible difference. At the least, we'd definitely make it there without risk of dropping dead. At the most, we'd have months or even years gained by spreading out the power, though he wasn't sure, despite being divided, how lessened it would be while still in close proximity.

Even with time, we had to successfully return the amulet. Two more people would die now if we didn't.

"Selk," Whistler whispered over his shoulder, "what's your seat number?"

"Twenty-one E."

The corner of his mouth lifted into a smile. "Twenty-one D."

"Twenty-one F," Cliff muttered, ahead of Whistler in line, my father ahead of him.

So much for whispering. *This'll be interesting.*

Once it was finally time to board, I took a shaky breath as I climbed the steps to the plane. It was surreal. I was living my dream of going to Egypt and observing artifacts and tombs, but under incredulous circumstances with people I never would have imagined.

My father and Sheridan waded into a front row on the left, leaving me in a separate one between two Cyclopes. It'd been weird to meet an attractive guy with a paranormal secret, but even weirder for Cliff and Sheridan to suddenly have third eyes, better stamina and overnight healing powers. (Zahid had explained that since the guardian Selket was a healer, power from artifacts she'd guarded healed those granted with it while resting and sleeping, enhancing the body's natural recovery process.)

Taking a deep breath, I glanced at Cliff, who looked out the window as we waited for the plane to take off, then Whistler, who looked at me.

"You all right?" he asked.

I nodded and smiled, fighting the urge to grab his hand.

"Do you want the window seat, Selk?" Cliff added. "Since you've never been on a plane before."

I rolled my eyes, just a little, because I knew Cliff had other motives than consideration for wanting to swap seats. "I'm good. I'll probably sleep most of the flight. I stayed up most of last night, packing and doing other last-minute stuff." Like calling Brandie and Lynette to let them know I wouldn't be in school for a while. That hadn't been easy. It'd taken me forever just to get them off the topic of Whistler and why on earth I'd go for a guy like that when Cliff was tall, dark and supposedly utterly dreamy.

In summary, they, like everyone else (except for my long-lost father) didn't approve of Whistler, but I did, and that was all that mattered to me.

Explaining my would-be absence had been even harder. Via a three-way phone convo, I told them about my father showing up and taking me to Egypt, but left it at that. I didn't know if they'd ever be able to handle the details. "If... *when* I get back, we'll talk more." Before they could protest, I'd said, "I love you guys," and hung up.

To make sure my mind wouldn't drift back to Post World, I turned to Whistler for conversation. "So how did you get into boxing?"

He glanced at me, then shrugged at the random question. "I got in a lot of fights when I first started out on my own. Then I saw a boxing match on television one day and figured I might as well be getting paid for fighting instead of getting sent to juvenile detention. Luckily, I figured that out before I turned eighteen." He glanced at me again before continuing, and Cliff made a scoffing sound. "I probably would have gotten thrown in jail and stayed there."

I frowned. "So you have no clue who your birth parents are?"

"No clue," he repeated. "Don't really care."

Biting my lip, I lowered my voice. "Well, why did the amulet's power give you mild amnesia while Cliff and Sheridan still have all their memories?"

"Maybe the amount of power absorbed decreases with each new person."

We fell silent for a little while, Cliff staring out the window as if trying to avoid even looking at Whistler.

"You know," Whistler said, "it was fun for a while, but I'm starting to get over the whole boxing thing. Especially since it hasn't been much of a challenge with my healing advantage."

"Are you going to quit?"

"Maybe. I don't know. I've never really sat down and thought about life, I guess. Hobbies, careers. They never stuck in my mind."

I smiled, fighting the urge to hold his hand harder than ever. "I always knew I wanted to be an Egyptologist and archaeologist. Boxing came later, and I never dreamed of going pro."

He laughed once. "Pro or not, I'm just sick of having to be around the lowlifes from Man Cave."

I laughed too. "Yeah, I kind of got that when you turned a two-man match into a five-man brawl. What did Varley say to you to make you want to punch his guts out?" Cliff leaned his head back against his headrest and closed his eyes as if I'd actually buy that he was going to sleep.

Whistler leaned toward me and murmured, "He saw or heard about us hanging out."

I arched a brow. "And that's so terrible why…?"

"He wanted to know your name. Said he never hooked up with girls he didn't know, and you'd be begging to hook up with him after he knocked out Appleton." He turned away, growling, "Arrogant son of a…"

Whistler clinched his jaw, but I just rolled my eyes. "I've learned to ignore guys like that."

"I haven't."

I rested my head on his shoulder and breathed him in, a clean scent that reminded me of fresh canvas, minus the blood and sweat. He put his arm around me. I closed my eyes. He placed his free hand on mine. We fell asleep as if no one could see us clinging to each other as if we wouldn't be coming back from Egypt.

* * * *

When I woke up, the memories came back fast. Where I was? Why I was there? Whose shoulder had I'd fallen asleep on? Something wasn't right. I remembered laying my head on Whistler's right shoulder, but I was now snuggled up to a left one.

"Good mor… What time is it?"

Cliff smiled. "Back in Snow Hill it's afternoon, but on this side of the world, it's about ten p.m."

I still didn't know how Zahid had managed to make arrangements for all of us, but I was sure buying off a lot of people played a big part in it. On the drive to the airport, he'd filled us in on a few more things, including how he'd supported himself by selling dormant artifacts the family had collected (and returned to Post World) over the years.

He'd pretty much gone broke with this last mission with the amulet, investing every last dime into seeing it carried through. For instance, getting Cliff and Sheridan last-minute shots required for international travel and forging papers to make it look as if they'd gotten them weeks before. Maybe even paying off people to give up their seats.

As for Whistler and I, we'd already been vaccinated years ago without even knowing it (though Zahid had prepared backup papers for us as well, just in case any of the vaccinations had expired). His foster parents and my mom had done it as a precaution, knowing we'd eventually have to go to Egypt. Zahid's initial attempts to return the amulet had been incredibly vain, because even if he'd been successful, Whistler would have still had power.

"Where's Whistler?" I asked.

"With your dad," Sheridan, in Whistler's seat, said. "Zahid already filled in Cliff and me about what sort of things to look out for in this Post World place while you were sleeping. Now he's giving Whistler some tips." Whistling low, he added, "Some freaky stuff."

Glancing at the front of the plane, I could just make out Whistler's dirty-blond hair through the rows of passengers. "Great," I muttered. "I'm the last to know."

I wriggled past Sheridan and then headed down the aisle. Whistler and Zahid were engrossed in hushed conversation, taking care to whisper so the sleeping middle-school-aged boy stuck in the window seat in their row wouldn't awaken and overhear.

When they didn't look up at my approach, I cleared my throat and spoke loudly. "Thanks for letting me sleep, but…" I chose my words carefully. "I might need to know about the tourist spots we'll be covering. You know, what to look for and what sights we'll probably be seeing."

Whistler smiled at me before nodding to Zahid, then he got up and walked to our row. I bit my tongue to stifle a laugh. He'd be squished between Cliff and Sheridan until I got back. I hoped a three-man fight wouldn't break out.

"So you think the guys can handle it?" I asked as I took Whistler's seat, my voice low.

Zahid nodded. "The boys are strong, and so are you."

Relieved at his confidence in us, though I didn't show it, I asked, "What, exactly, do we have to face?"

"Animate artifacts and pottery that can't shatter, passageways that can sense your presence, ancient creatures that carried their appetites into the next dimension."

He glanced around before continuing, finding that all the nearby passengers either had on headphones or were asleep. "And mummies. Don't be deceived by their brittle appearance. They can slow you in your tracks until they're able to catch you. Stay as far away from them as you can, and, if possible, avoid them at all costs."

"What, like slow-motion?" I shook my head in disbelief. "So are these creatures, artifacts and mummies punch-able and kickable?"

He nodded. "It's better to outrun them. Choosing your battles is the key to survival in Post World. If you can sneak up on a mummy, attack it and bring it down. There's little you can do once it has you in its sights— fighting or running won't help." After a pause, he said, "As for the artifacts, it's best to avoid those as well. They can't be destroyed, and they can break your bones. Your grandfather fractured his ribs and broke his elbow once. I myself have broken a leg or two."

I felt the blood rush out of my face, probably pooling with the dread in my stomach.

"However many we've lost in Post World over time," he added, "we've managed to return every artifact. Otherwise, you and I wouldn't be here today. Our ancestors would have dropped dead, ending the chain of Selket's descendants."

"Have descendants of any other gods or goddesses become..." I searched for the right word, "extinct?"

"I'm not sure." He paused, letting me process the information. "I'll be picking up a guidebook that's been created by and passed down to generations of Selket's descendants." He sat thinking for a moment before he added, "The crocodile beings. If you can tame them, they'll let you leave the pool room."

"Pool room?" My mind swimming with confusion, I muttered, "I hope this book has a map."

"That it does," Zahid said. "I know you've studied Egyptology, but while some knowledge may help, it's probably best you forget what you've learned and replace it with the contents of the guidebook." When I nodded, he continued. "The pool room is vast and filled with the venom Selket banished from victims in her lifetime, mostly from serpents and scorpions. The crocodiles are immune to it, but it'll kill humans."

At my gasp, the little boy next to Zahid stirred. Once I was sure he wouldn't wake up, I asked, "Did you tell the guys about taming crocodiles?"

Zahid nodded. "They were more concerned with the mummies and the awkward layout of Post World itself. It's easy to become lost and separated, so stay with each other at all times. Don't be tempted to split up in hopes of dodging obstacles or saving time." He paused a moment to let everything sink in, then said, "There isn't much more I can tell you without the book. With that, I'll be able to go over everything with you and the young men in detail. I can give you a general description of Selket's Post World. It's comprised of four popular sites known in Egypt—the Temple of Horus, the three largest pyramids at Giza—the Pyramid of Khafre, the Pyramid of Menkaure and the Great Pyramid of Khufu—the palace of Ramses III and Herodotus' Egyptian Labyrinth beside what Herodotus called the City of Crocodiles, which turned into the pool room in Post World."

My eyes widened. I'd read about all those places, but the last one in particular astounded me. "The Labyrinth? That's pretty much as visible as Atlantis. I know Egyptologists think they've found it, but it's buried under centuries of sand."

Zahid smiled a little. "I'm happy you're enthusiastic about your birth country."

I paused a long moment, having difficulty processing what he'd just said. "My birth country? I was born in America, in Snow Hill." He slowly shook his head. "That's impossible," I protested. "You left Mom and me the day after I was born. Didn't you flee the States?"

"I left, but your mother stayed with your grandparents at their home in Egypt until you two were able to go back to Maryland. In fact, that was only weeks before they too returned to the States, Nebraska, and fostered Whistler, who was a toddler."

I sat back in my seat, facing the row ahead of me. After a while, I said, my voice barely audible, "So you only tell me this now when a lot of us could die."

"I'll tell you everything you want to know about your Egyptian family once we're safely back in the United States. No one will die, Selk. I'm positive."

My face numbing at the revelations, I took a shaky breath and forced myself to push anything that didn't directly involve Post World to the back of my mind. As Zahid had said, there would be plenty of time for family-related questions. Though I wasn't as confident as he was that we'd be coming back.

"The Labyrinth," I said again, as if we'd never strayed off topic. "Will it look like it does on Earth? As in, pretty much invisible?"

"Nothing in Post World will be the same as it is on Earth. Everything will appear new, as if back in time, and yet, time there is the same as on Earth. There will be no dust, and the painted walls and jewels will be as bold and glittering as they were millennia ago. So you'll walk through the sites as they appeared when they were first built. Only, the magic of Post World will distort them." He paused as if gathering his thoughts. "I've never been good at describing things, especially the extraordinary. Post World is a place that's best interpreted for oneself."

Feeling sick to my stomach from equal excitement and dread, I muttered, "Lovely. Any other vital advice before I go back to my seat?"

"All the landmarks are unnaturally connected. On maps they appear in a straight line, but if you exit the labyrinth, you'll return to where you began, the Temple of Horus."

"So that's all there is to the world? An infinite loop of the same places?"

"Not a loop," he corrected, "but a line like a loop. I don't understand how it works, but that's how it is." As I stood, he added, "Again, the guidebook will help, but mostly, you and the young men will learn as you travel through Post World yourselves. Reading and studying can only teach you so much."

On the verge of a headache, I nodded before walking back to my original seat. At first, I'd been worried if I'd remember everything. Now I didn't see how things that surreal were possible to forget.

* * * *

Luxor International Airport was vast and boxy. When Zahid led us to grab our luggage, I fidgeted. Way too soon, we'd be in Post World.

"You all right?" Whistler asked. As I nodded, he added, "Can I talk to you for a sec?"

"Sure," I said, taking a deep breath to calm my nerves.

After I followed him behind a glowing map of the airport, he blurted, "I think we should tell them."

I blinked, taken aback. "Tell them what?"

"About us."

"Why?"

"Because I can't grab your hand and hold you and tell you it's going to be okay if we're trying to keep this secret. And I need to do that."

I smiled. "No, you don't."

"Yes," he insisted, his face serious, "I do."

I was sure everyone was already suspicious about us, but I still braced myself for their reactions. Zahid was the first one to see us holding hands. He was on the phone, but he just smiled at us and kept on talking as if he lived with Mom and I, and Whistler had been coming over every weekend for dinner.

"One down," I whispered.

Sheridan saw us next. For a moment, I thought he was going to grin, but instead, he gaped at us, gesturing to Cliff with his eyes.

His back to us, Cliff had to turn before he saw us. Though he'd seen me run crying to Whistler at the gym and fall asleep on his shoulder, there must have been something official about seeing us now, holding each other's hand so intentionally.

He gaped at us in horror. His knuckles flexed.

"Cliff, I lied," I admitted.

"Everything's happened fast," Whistler said, "but Selk and I have something really special, and we think it's stupid to hide it anymore, especially with everything going on."

Cliff stared Whistler down for a full ten seconds. At first, I thought he really was going to punch him, but he just stormed past us, not looking at Whistler or even me. I was probably the only girl in America whose father approved of the guy she liked when her personal trainer didn't.

"I'm going to talk to him," Sheridan said after a few seconds, his voice low.

Even he wasn't showing his usual indifference. I hoped we hadn't just broken up the team we so desperately needed in order to survive.

After about ten minutes, Zahid got a phone call, then told us we needed to head outside. In the dark, it was way colder than I'd expected, even in my sweater. Zahid looked a little chilled as well, but the guys—presumably via their Cyclops powers—seemed unaffected.

Whistler stepped closer and pulled me into him, and I snuggled against him as I took in the landscape. The buildings and earth were sand-colored even in the dark.

It was only a couple minutes before Zahid got up and announced that the big SUV that pulled up in front of the airport was our ride. It parked a little way off from the entrance, behind a series of taxis, and an older woman in a landscape-colored dress and bright turban stepped out from the passenger side.

As she approached, Whistler tensed beside me. When I glanced up, I saw his jaw had tightened. Then I knew who the woman was.

She smiled broadly and kissed either side of Zahid's face before approaching the rest of us, stopping in front of Whistler and me. "My dear boy," she said, her accent thicker than Zahid's, "I thank you for coming here. Forgive me?"

Whistler said nothing, just held me tighter, so she smiled sadly and turned to me. "Dear Selk, I knew you would grow into a lovely young woman." She paused, then asked the same question, whispering this time as if her confidence had faded. "Forgive me?"

That was such a huge question. I hesitated, knowing what she and my grandfather had done to Whistler, but I also knew they'd been keeping the family's best interest in mind.

Glancing at Zahid, whose eyes shone with pride, I said, "I think I can. In time."

She smiled wider and clasped her hands. "So very brave, all of you. When Zahid told me you and Whistler had found each other, I didn't believe him at first. How can I deny my own eyes?"

Cliff, standing a little way off, coughed sarcastically. She walked over and patted his hand, then repeated the process with Sheridan. "Thank you, both. Very brave young men."

"*Ummi*, we need to go," Zahid said. My grandmother nodded, then gestured for us to follow her to the car.

"Fadila," Whistler said. He glanced at me and waited until she faced him before continuing. "I forgive you."

She ran back to us, and I stepped aside so she could hug Whistler, who swallowed hard. I blinked back tears. The sight was as touching as it was strange. Whistler had known my grandmother's name before I did.

The SUV had three rows of seats. I sat with Zahid in the second row, and the guys, much to their irritation, piled into the back. Driving was, apparently, my grandfather, a quiet, stony-faced man who'd greeted us all, but had said little else than his name, Naim.

"Shouldn't we be going over the guidebook?" I asked as we pulled out of the airport.

"No," Fadila said. "I want it to be fresh on your mind when you enter Post World. Don't worry. We'll waste no time. The supplies you'll need are in the trunk—rope, water bottles and things of that sort."

Naim said something in Arabic, and Fadila shook her head before replying. "No. We'll go straight to the temple. We can't waste time." She turned in her seat toward us before adding, "The Temple of Horus is about an hour-and-a-half's drive from here. That is the entrance to Selket's Post World."

I stared out the window, watching the sandy landscape briefly shift to patches of color as we drove through a market area. We passed a massive hotel or two—even they were the color of pale sand—and I squinted to make out ancient temples and architecture in the distance. Occasionally, I caught glimpses of the River Nile.

The drive, even with the surprising number of cars on the road for that time of night (or morning) felt more like thirty minutes.

As we neared Edfu, Zahid broke the silence. "*Ummi*, shouldn't Selk and the young men start reviewing the guidebook?"

"Not just yet. Fresh on the mind, remember?" Fadila glanced at me in the rearview mirror. "You're so much like my Qubilah. Did Zahid tell you of your aunt?"

I nodded. "Yeah. I'm really sorry."

Fadila smiled sadly. "So beautiful, so determined. Much like you." She glanced at Zahid. "Your father brings her back to me through you."

I fidgeted in my seat, feeling awkward. I'd never met my aunt and had barely met my grandparents, and my grandma was talking as if we'd been hanging out my whole life. Luckily, we shortly pulled up to the temple, so I didn't have to think too long about whether I should have replied or not.

I gaped at the smooth, gargantuan structure. It was decorated with embossed silhouettes of ancient Egyptians. Guarding the lofty entrance were two falcon statues made from what looked like granite. In the distant darkness, just behind the entrance, I thought I saw soaring columns and more vast passageways.

"Welcome to Edfu," Naim muttered, taking me by surprise.

"Welcome to the Temple of Horus," Fadila clarified.

As we drew nearer, I saw how bulky and blocky the structure was. From the front, it gave the illusion of one thin wall when it was actually comprised of several thick walls that stretched across acres.

For one moment, I allowed myself to give in to my inner Egyptology nerd and marvel at the sight. "It's amazing," I breathed, determined to get out of Post World alive.

Once we came back, I'd find a camera somewhere and take as many videos and pictures as the memory card would hold, maybe even ask Zahid if we could detour at the pyramids and sphinx. Assuming the alternate-Egypt experience of Post World wouldn't scar all of us, physically and emotionally.

There was no one there this time of night, save for two men in traditional Egyptian garb—turbans and loose robes. Naim parked a little way off from them, dust rising and settling by the tires.

"Who are they?" I asked.

"Dragomen," Fadila answered. "Egyptian tour guides, whom we also know personally. They know of Post World, though they aren't descendants of any ancient Egyptian figures. They'll help us better inform you of your mission, as well as details about Selket herself."

I narrowed my eyes in suspicion. "What else is there to know besides the guidebook?"

"There is always more to know," Naim muttered, then opened the driver's door. Once Fadila got out, Zahid and I opened our own doors, and the guys in the backseat followed us onto the sand.

I narrowed my eyes when the men didn't move, just stood a way from the entrance, staring, waiting. Waiting for what? For us to gather our things?

"I thought we'd be alone," Zahid said, echoing my thoughts.

"We can use all the help we can get," Fadila remarked, opening the back of the SUV. "The two will help them into Post World."

Zahid fell silent in thought, then nodded with a smile. "Always so thoughtful, *Ummi*."

"Where is the amulet, my son?" Naim asked. "I'll distribute power to them while you help the group gather their things."

When Zahid handed him the amulet, I finally saw it in detail for the first time in person. It was larger than I'd assumed, about the size of my hand. It hung from a multi-colored, multi-strand beaded chain, painted a turquoise-blue color that had chipped and faded with age. The dark outline of the eye was still bold, even the traditional Egyptian eye-makeup line that slanted and curved beneath it.

I watched as Naim walked toward the two dragomen and took them behind a wall—should anyone have driven up, I assumed—before accepting a backpack from Fadila. She handed Whistler, Sheridan and Cliff each one before gesturing for us to follow her to the temple.

"Where's the guidebook?" I asked. "When are we—"

"Naim has it," Fadilla interrupted. "We'll review it in the temple. The information must be as fresh on your minds as possible."

Zahid looked ahead, but I exchanged glances with the guys, who appeared as bewildered as me. "Yeah, I get that," I said, "but it's not like we have short-term memory."

Fadila kept walking in silence, straight between the falcon statues. I hesitated as Zahid followed her. With the walls blocking the little moonlight there was, it was way too dark inside for my taste.

Swallowing hard, I wondered aloud, "Is Post World going to be this dark?" If it was scary now on non-magical Earth, what would it be like to fight mummies and other deadly creatures in limited light?

"Not all parts," Zahid said over his shoulder, pausing in the entrance.

"And there are flashlights in your backpacks," Fadila added, though I couldn't see her.

I jumped when someone grabbed my hand from behind, then relaxed at Whistler's voice. "We'll all be together," he murmured. "And I'm not leaving your side."

I squeezed his hand and took a step backward, closer to him. Zahid had disappeared into the temple, and Fadila pressed, "Coming?"

"Yeah," I replied, my voice shaky. "We're right behind you."

Whistler and I, hand in hand, stepped into the temple with Cliff and Sheridan close behind, but shadows and columns and sandy walls were all I could see.

"Zahid? Fadila?" They couldn't have disappeared.

Light exploded somewhere ahead, the same colorless light that had paralyzed Whistler back in Snow Hill. It wriggled, a bright floating blob, beckoning.

"Fadila?" I repeated.

A few moments passed before she said, "To the light."

We walked to the blob, which was suspended in midair between two of the temple's massive columns. I'd half-expected the portal to give a preview of what lay on the other side like in some fantasy and sci-fi movies, but it was one of those enter-at-your-own-risk types, like picking a door at random on a game show. Only, we had one door to choose from with one of two prizes to win—death or life.

Fadila stepped out from behind a column, tapping an old journal-sized book against her hand. "In you go," she said, taking me by surprise.

Cliff spoke this time. "Where are the others? Selk's father and the dragomen?"

"Naim is with them." We stared at Fadila, but she offered nothing further.

That's when I started panicking.

Dropping Whistler's hand, I stepped toward her. "Okay, *what* is going on?" She smiled a little, glancing to her right. I followed her gaze.

In a dark corner, I could just distinguish four silhouettes. Naim stood off to himself while the two dragomen restrained Zahid, their hands clamped over his mouth as he struggled to speak.

I gasped, my hands shaking. "Zahid!" The guys sprinted with me across the uneven temple floor.

Naim, in no shape to attempt to stop me, retreated to Fadila, and I managed to kick and punch Zahid free.

"Selk, we need to leave," he said, helping me tie up the dazed dragomen with their own turbans.

"What about Post World?"

"We'll figure that out later," he said, his eyes wide with shock. "*Ummi, Abbi...* I can't believe it. They had no intention of sending the dragomen to help you."

"Yeah, I get that," I said before spinning around. I gasped. Several more dragomen had appeared from behind walls and columns. The guys did some damage to a few, but there were too many for even professional boxers to handle.

"Selk!" Either Whistler, Cliff or both called.

Zahid grabbed my arm to stop me from running to them, but I shook it off and sprinted just as four dragomen threw Sheridan into the portal. "No!" I screamed, picking up my pace again after stumbling on a chipped block of sandstone. Cliff head-butted one of the men before they threw him in after Sheridan, leaving only Whistler in the temple.

"Selk!" Zahid called from behind me. "Don't follow them. You're unprepared!"

"*They* are unprepared!" I shouted, skidding to a halt just out of reach of the dragomen, weighing my options. Whistler struggled to break free by the portal. If we didn't go in, we'd die. If we did go in unprepared, we'd probably die. Probably was better than definitely.

I glanced at Fadila, who stood smiling with Naim a little way from the portal. She still tapped the guidebook in her hand. It, reviewed or not, was our only hope.

When Whistler went in, I knew it was only a matter of time before the men caught and outnumbered me. We all had backpacks with supplies, so I just had to time getting that book right.

After throwing a side kick at a dragoman who'd approached me, I sprinted toward Fadila, whose eyes hardened as she realized what I was after. She smiled again, and shortly, I was knocked down by multiple men, my chin ramming into the hard ground. Ignoring the pain, I thrashed and screamed as they grabbed me and drug me backward to the portal. Naim remained silent, but Fadila laughed.

"A daughter for a daughter, Zahid!"

So that was what this was about. She blamed Zahid for my aunt's death, and she wanted revenge, even if getting it meant the deaths of not only him and me, but also her and Naim.

I couldn't see Zahid, but the moment before the dragomen hurled me backward into the paralyzing portal, I heard him shout, "Selk, catch!" The guidebook tangled with the amulet, spiraled toward me like a football. I managed to pull it with me before the voices and laughter and dragomen disappeared, leaving nothing but empty, stunning light.

SITE FOUR: SELKET'S POST WORLD
CHAPTER SEVEN

Slow Echoes

I fell backward, but I hit something that flipped me around, causing me to land on my chin again. This time, I felt a thread of blood when I lifted my head. My groans echoed in the new space, which was just a bit lighter than the dark temple in Edfu.

Though I hadn't lost consciousness, I was still having trouble gathering my thoughts. They returned, but slowly. The book. The guys. The amulet. I needed to find all of them. Zahid had said the first place in Post World was the alternate version of Horus' Temple, so they had to have landed nearby.

"Selk! Guys, she's over here!"

I'd never been so happy to hear Sheridan's voice. I got to my knees, my backpack feeling heavier than it was, and wiped the blood from my chin. The large tan bricks in the floor blurred for a couple seconds, then cleared.

"B...book," I muttered as their footsteps echoed near. "Where's the book?" Cliff and Whistler helped me up, and after regaining my balance, I hugged both of their waists. "I'm so sorry. I had no idea. Zahid didn't even know."

"It's all right," Cliff said.

"We had to come here regardless," Whistler added. "We just have to figure things out for ourselves now."

"I got it!" Sheridan appeared from behind a column a couple seconds later, holding up the guidebook. "It was wedged against that column. Must have been some landing."

"Are you guys all right?" I asked, glancing at each of them, who seemed unharmed.

"Yeah, those guys didn't know how to throw a punch," Sheridan said.

Whistler pulled me away from Cliff and touched my chin. Fresh blood glistened on his fingers. "We need to get you patched up and take a moment to think before we attempt anything."

"There's probably first aid and Band-Aids in the backpacks," I said. "Fadila told the truth about that much." I shrugged my backpack off and dug through it until I found a Band-Aid. Whistler took it from me and then put it on my drizzling chin.

"Sheridan," I said, stepping toward him, "did you see the amulet anywhere?" When his face paled, I searched Cliff's and Whistler's faces, panicked. "Guys?"

Whistler stepped to my side and took my hand. "Cliff and I ran after whoever—or whatever—it was, but he disappeared down a darker passage in the temple."

"We'll find it," Cliff reassured. "They couldn't have gotten far."

I gaped at them. "We're supposed to be the only ones here. Did a dragoman absorb some power and follow us, after all?"

"Fadila probably wanted to make sure we don't succeed," Whistler muttered.

"Or my aunt isn't so dead." I couldn't remember if the guys had heard about my aunt or not, so I told them how Fadila blamed Zahid for her death. Now we were trapped in Post World with no idea where or how to get out or even navigate, and it was because of me.

Averting my eyes, I muttered, "So I'm doubly responsible for dragging you guys into this. Our lives are at stake not only because of my relation to Selket, but because my grandmother wants me dead to make my father suffer like she did. No apology from me can fix that."

"Selk," Cliff said, grabbing my shoulders to turn me toward him, "I came here by choice, and so did Sheridan. We want to help you."

"I would have come even if I'd had a choice," Whistler added.

Cliff narrowed his eyes a bit, but fought off the irritation and squeezed my arm. "Let's find that amulet."

I glanced around, truly taking in my surroundings for the first time. The columns and bricks and decorations were identical to the real temple, but there was no dust. Even though limestone wasn't exactly known for glistening, everything seemed to shine and pop with the newness of a freshly built structure.

Taking the guidebook from Sheridan's hand, I said, "We need to read first."

Cliff furrowed his brows. "Why would someone take the amulet but leave the guidebook? If they really wanted us dead, they'd have taken both."

I opened the book, careful not to tear its old, fragile pages. "They must have fallen far apart. Whoever took the amulet probably had little time to grab the book and outrun you guys."

The first four pages were maps—more like diagrams—of the four structures of Selket's Post World. The details were intimidating, seeming more like blueprints for a rocket scientist.

"It looks like the temple is the smallest of the structures." My eyes widened as I glanced at the high roof and the enormous columns. "Or at least the shortest distance to cross."

Whistler looked at every wall, turning in a slow circle, then said, "There are several passages. I can't see the entrance to the pyramids, but the ones to the left are dead ends, just chambers or something. We need to walk forward for a while and then turn right."

"Okay, so we leave the temple, but then what?" I'd been confident before, but now, I felt as if someone had blindfolded me. "When or *if* we find the amulet, where do we return it so it falls dormant? Zahid warned us about each part of Post World, but he never said where to leave the amulet. He just told us where the end is, and even then, he said we're pretty much walking in circles without circles back to the beginning."

"Selk." I was startled by the seriousness in Sheridan's voice. "If there is anything fighting has taught me, it's to not ask how or why or when or where. It's to *fight*. Just fight until you know it's over. I have a feeling this place is like that. When it's over, when we find the way home, we'll know."

I nodded slowly, taken aback by the wisdom of Sheridan's words. "You know, that actually makes sense. Even Zahid said that reading and studying can only teach you so much. Maybe the guidebook really is just hints."

I flipped through the guidebook, which seemed to be in order of the four structures. The section for the temple was the shortest, with nothing but physical descriptions of the columns and bricked floors.

"I think the temple is our checkpoint. There are no warnings about it in here. So if we're in trouble, we just need to either retrace our steps or keep pushing forward until it loops around again." I looked at the wall behind me. Unlike the real temple, no falcon statues guarded an entrance. "Can you see the labyrinth through there?"

The guys studied the wall, but eventually shook their heads and shrugged. "Nothing but the wall you see," Whistler said.

"So to the pyramids it is then," I said. "If we find the amulet thief, maybe we can ask where to return it."

"Or threaten," Cliff said.

"Yeah," I muttered, nodding. "Most likely."

Without looking at the guys, I set off through the temple, clutching the guidebook with both hands. As we walked, I found it strange how similar Post World's temple was to the real one. It seemed as if the farther we ventured, more and more differences appeared. Some places in the roof and even walls should have revealed the near-dawn sky on Earth, but the structure we walked through was sealed and contained more chambers than I remembered studying.

It was a surprisingly peaceful first fifteen minutes or so of walking, as if we were just kids on a fieldtrip, but after following a long stretch of wall and hieroglyphics, an open chamber to my left caught my eye. Not the surplus jewels or pottery or figurines, but the silhouette. A large, golden silhouette painted with stunning details, lying still in open-eyed slumber.

The sight was so stereotypical, I couldn't stop my eyes from widening. I walked toward it.

"Selk, what is it?" Cliff asked.

I didn't answer, just ran my hand over the golden face, the dark cone beard. "So not right."

Whistler walked to my side, realization dawning on him. "Dude. I'm no expert in Egyptology, but shouldn't Tut's sarcophagus be in a pyramid or something?"

"No, the Valley of the Kings in Luxor. A small tomb underground. It was believed to have been an unexpected death, so there was no time to prepare."

I studied the ancient coffin, noticing how much it gleamed in the dim light. Nothing ancient about it. "Definitely not in the Temple of Horus. I'm not even sure if they were constructed in the same time period." Dates were the worst part about studying Egyptology. They all seemed to blur together, as if Cleopatra had been Tutankhamen's neighbor.

Something besides the random placement of Tut's alternate tomb tugged at my mind. Searching the room, I wondered aloud, "Guys, shouldn't we be in pitch blackness? Where's that light coming from?"

Squinting, I looked everywhere, up and down and side to side, but saw no lamps or candles. I noticed at the bottom of each wall was the faintest crease like a thread. A golden glow seeped through, so subtly it was frightening. If this place could hide light so easily, what else could jump out at us?

After tracing the glow, I shuddered at the thought and forced myself to leave Tut's sarcophagus.

I was a few paces away from the tomb when Sheridan asked, "Uh... guys, should we find this weird?" He'd walked into Tut's chamber and studied the end of the coffin.

I joined the others, who studied with him. "What is it?"

"It's open a little," Whistler said.

"Like someone was searching for loot and forgot to close it," Sheridan added.

Or maybe," Cliff said, starting to look freaked out, "like someone *left* and forgot to close it." He swallowed hard. The heavy top grated as he slid it back just enough to look inside, revealing no bandages or corpses or even artifacts.

"You can't possibly think a mummy stole the amulet," I said, though my voice was soft with uncertainty.

"Remember what your dad said about these mummies," Sheridan reminded. "They don't sound brittle and helpless."

I scanned the wall of hieroglyphics and traditional Egyptian paintings behind Tut's sarcophagus, settling on an image of a young woman in the left corner. She wore a headdress and jewelry and other Egyptian garb, but something about her didn't *feel* Egyptian. Maybe it was because, though everything seemed new there, her image stood out like a renovated room. Walking closer, I could almost smell a fresh coat of the powdery pigment the Egyptians had used to paint.

"What the..." I stopped inches in front of her, studying her complexion. It was even lighter than mine, ivory with just a hint of exotic heritage.

Stranger even were her astonishing blue eyes and dark red hair.

My hand trembling, I reached up to touch the painting. It smudged. "I think our thief is also an artist." Turning toward the others, I showed them the chalky red coloring on my fingertips.

Cliff was about to comment when we all jerked our heads toward a muffled yelp coming from a farther passage in the temple. The guys and I took off without a word. The passage grew narrower the farther we ran. Eventually, we had to run single file, Cliff in the lead and Sheridan at the end behind me.

"Do you guys see anything?" I whispered, keeping pace.

"A figure to the right up ahead," Cliff said, "but it's still pretty far away."

"Well, sprint!" I hissed.

We ran past a few more odd rooms before turning right. The path widened, but the rooms ended. When gold flashed and waved a little way ahead, I thought the light in the floors was just getting brighter, but Cliff shouted something and sped up.

Everything changed.

We climbed a rugged amethyst staircase that probably would have been dusty and lined with rails on Earth from modern excavators. The walls here were solid turquoise.

The gold light still shone, but had faded a bit, like afternoon turning to dusk. We didn't need flashlights yet. I just hoped it wouldn't get any darker.

The staircase led us to a small room with the entrances of two new staircases, the right going up and the left going down. Artifacts glittered in the dim light—jewelry, trinkets, pottery and gargantuan raw gems. A thief's dream.

Good thing we knew better. Taking a dormant artifact from Earth was one thing, but taking an artifact already returned to Post World was another. I didn't want to find out what sort of consequences that would lead to.

"We're in the first pyramid, Khafre," I said, looking at the maps in the guidebook. "This is the largest of the three, and it has tons of passages weaving together that I can't make out. Can you guys see anything?"

A noise like pottery crashing came from the left passage. Cliff's neon eye squinted, then disappeared before he took off down the left staircase, his backpack knocking over a basket. Sheridan followed, but as he disappeared, I noticed the basket didn't stop trembling from the fall. One by one, the other artifacts followed suit until the whole room shivered and the temperature grew unusually cool.

"Come on, guys!" Sheridan called. "We can't get separated!"

I hesitated, struggling to make out pictures and Egyptian captions in Khafre's section in the guidebook. A few had been translated in English and a couple other languages.

"Don't touch," I read aloud, looking at Whistler. "I don't understand. What do we not—"

"Selk, look out!" Whistler grabbed my arm and yanked me into the right passage just before the roof collapsed and filled the room with artifacts, sealing us in. The light was even dimmer there. Through the clamor, I heard Cliff's and Sheridan's muffled shouts from the next staircase.

"Are you okay?" Whistler asked, scanning the amethyst steps.

"Yeah," I said. "What about Cliff and Sheridan? Do you see them?"

"They're below us, not too far ahead."

"Then let's go. We'll probably catch up to them when the passages open up." With nowhere to go but forward, I jogged up the staircase, beginning to see why Zahid had said agility was key to surviving Post World.

"Selk," Whistler said, jogging behind me, "the artifacts are still rattling."

The moment I glanced over my shoulder, a vase leaped from the pile at the former entrance to our staircase and glided in a comet-fast arch toward Whistler's head.

"Duck!" I shouted, grabbing his hand and yanking him down to let the vase fly over us.

It didn't even shatter on landing. Keeping Whistler's hand, I jumped over the three-foot-tall artifact and sprinted forward, more pottery and jewels rattling in our wake. Whistler let go of my hand to kick a carnelian basket back, and I unsuccessfully attempted to dodge a downpour of gold wrist cuffs and multi-jeweled pendants. The force of the blows was stronger than I'd expected, as if the artifacts were being thrown from the walls rather than merely falling.

As we neared the top of the staircase, the ceiling inclined to four times its previous height. More artifacts spilled, leaping toward the entrance like frogs.

"Whistler, hurry! We'll never get out of here!" My lungs sobbed from sprinting up the long staircase, but I forced myself to run even faster.

Something came out of nowhere, a large bowl or plate, that slammed into my face and sent me stumbling backward, knocking Whistler over. We skidded to a stop a couple steps down. I blinked heavily.

"Selk?"

The blow having stunned me, I couldn't think to answer Whistler. The entrance ahead, though lofty, was filling fast as the artifacts kept falling in the same spot.

Whistler pulled us both up and somehow managed to squeeze past me so he could take my hand and pull me along. I stumbled after him, shaking my head to clear my vision. With a strong kick, he shortened the pile just enough for us to crawl over. It bobbed in protest with our weight, nearly throwing us off balance.

We stumbled onto the other side and were seconds past the entrance when a section of roof behind us caved in, creating a wall impossible to kick down.

We ran for a few seconds more and then made a left, then right turn before stopping. Both of us panting, I listened for more metallic trembling, but the only thing I heard was the ringing in my ears. Still feeling unsteady, I leaned against the wall and grabbed my head, thankful to still be alive after that blow.

"Selk." Whistler put his hands on my shoulders. "Are you okay?"

"Tell Cliff that if I can take a punch from a metal plate," I said, "I can certainly take a punch from one of you guys."

"Sit down for a minute. There are no artifacts in this room, just hieroglyphics."

With no desire to argue, I leaned against my backpack and slid down the wall, gold like the ceiling. The floor, also gold, moved a little in front of me as I did, so I put my head between my knees and took several deep breaths.

Whistler slid down next to me and then put his arm around my shoulders. After a few seconds, I turned toward him and laid my head against his collarbone, my breaths only now slowing from our sprint up the stairs.

"I'm glad you're here," I whispered. "I don't think I could have made it this far without you."

"You would have had Cliff and Sheridan," he said. "I haven't done anything but watch you get a concussion. Some boyfriend I am."

I tilted my head up to look at him, butterflies swimming with the spots before my eyes. "We're boyfriend and girlfriend?"

He blinked, taken aback by his own words, then met my gaze. "Yeah, we are." Smiling, he added, "If you want to be."

Returning his smile, I said, "Duh," then kissed him lightly. "And I would have been part of that artifact wall at the first staircase entrance if you hadn't pulled me out of the way." I held his gaze for a moment, then looked down the long, tall passage. "We need to catch up to the others."

Whistler kept his hand on my arm, stopping me from getting up. "You need to sit here for another minute."

Reluctantly, I shook his hand off and started to stand. "I'm fine." He stood beside me, helping me up. "I assume being in Post World stops the danger of us falling dead any minute," I said, "but I don't know about Zahid. Plus, who knows when another ceiling could cave in." I opened the guidebook to the map of the Pyramid of Khafre, but my vision still danced a little, so I handed it to Whistler while I blinked several times.

"Looks like we're already approaching the Pyramid of Menkaure," he said. "It's just past this passage."

"The map of Khafre showed we'd reconnect with Sheridan and Cliff before then."

Whistler flipped between the two maps, then said, "Yeah, it does look like that. Unless the equilibriums of the pyramids run into each other, and that's how they're connected."

I thought about that for a second, mentally flipping through the random facts I'd come across when reading about archaeology and a little geology. "Yeah, that makes sense. Like the isostasy of an iceberg or mountain. Some is actually below the earth or water, and there are passages and rooms below ground even in the pyramids on Earth. Plus, I'm sure Selket wouldn't have guarded every room, which explains why the interiors of Post World are so jumbled and sometimes brief."

"So on to Menkaure then," Whistler said, leafing through the guidebook. "Let's see what dangers await us there." After a second, he stopped on a page, muttering, "What the..."

"What is it?"

"It's dark. A whole page was shaded with charcoal or something. Look."

He turned the book for me to see, and sure enough, half the map of the Pyramid of Menkaure was black. I swallowed hard. Darkness was fine. Things lurking in dark unknown territory was a different story.

Whistler studied the floor as we shrugged our backpacks off and then got flashlights. "I don't see Cliff or Sheridan," he said. "I can't see much of anything, actually. The glow is really faint in the passage below."

"It's not exactly bright here, either," I said, trying to keep myself from losing my nerve. "Any warnings we should keep in mind?"

I started to put my backpack back on, but he grabbed a strap from me. "I'll carry that until you feel better."

I narrowed my eyes and pulled the strap back, more amused by his sweetness than exasperated. "I said I'm fine. And I have no problem toting heavy things around. I work out, remember?" Winking, I clutched my flashlight and squeezed past him, leaving him with the guidebook, but he stopped me again.

"I'm at least going first this time," he said. "You could have been killed back there."

"You could have too," I argued.

"Yeah, but I heal freakishly fast, remember?"

Obliging him, I pressed myself against the wall so he could squeeze past. He paused, catching my gaze. My breath caught at being so close, but he turned away and continued on the path.

As we approached a door at the end, I admired the paintings on the golden walls. The more images I studied, the more confused I became. Something wasn't right. They were definitely Egyptian, ancient even, but not stereotypical. Biting my lip, I leaned against the left wall to study a painting on the right.

Whistler walked a couple steps before realizing I'd stopped, then joined me. "What's wrong?"

"These pictures," I said. "There's something about them I can't put my finger on…"

Most were people, ornately decorated, but a few shapes looked like arrows pointing toward the door we were about to enter. I traced my fingers over the wall. The images of the people stayed intact, but the arrows smudged and stuck to my skin.

My eyes widening, I exchanged glances with Whistler. "Fresh again," I said. "The thief must have come through here, not in Cliff and Sheridan's passage, after all."

"You think he or she is trying to tell us something?"

"I don't know," I said, then looked at the door. "There are no other warnings besides darkness for the next pyramid?"

"No," Whistler said, studying the book. "Just that dark page, but there are arrows…" He flipped between two pages. "The arrow on Khafre's map is pointing toward the door, and the arrow for Menkaure's map is pointing toward the darkness."

"So they'd be facing each other if the maps were joined."

"Yeah," he said. "Why—and how—is the same clue in the guidebook if the amulet thief just painted those arrows?"

I shook my head. "It has to have something to do with the darkness, a warning, but I don't know what it could be. Zahid was right. Most of Post World has to be figured out as you go." I glanced at the guidebook. "Especially with that vague instruction manual. My relatives were the worst note-takers ever."

"They were probably too busy running from animate pottery and mummies."

Something clicked in my brain when he said that. Looking at the paintings on the walls again, things were beginning to make sense. The figures weren't slender and angular like most ancient depictions of the Egyptians, but clunky and almost shapeless. Lifeless but beautiful.

"Sarcophaguses," I breathed. My heart breaking into a jog, I looked at the door. "And darkness."

"What is it?" Whistler grabbed my hand, searching my eyes.

"I don't know if Cliff and Sheridan can avoid them, but we have no choice."

At the word "them," realization dawned on his face. "Mummies," he muttered. "Of course. We're in the pyramids."

Panic clouded my mind. "What did Zahid say about the mummies again?"

"He said to stay far away from them and avoid them at all costs."

I laughed dryly. "Yeah. Good advice, Zahid. What else?"

"That they'll slow us down to catch us, and to choose our battles. I guess just use our judgment on when to run and when to fight."

I nodded, exhaling shakily. "Okay. We can do this. At least we know what we're facing."

"Thanks to you," he said, then took my other hand. "You afraid?"

I hesitated, then averted my eyes and admitted in a soft voice, "So scared I could cry."

"Me too." He pulled me into him and wrapped his arms around me, and I closed my eyes and breathed him in.

"I'm so glad I didn't get stuck with Sheridan," I murmured. "I'd hug a mummy before hugging him."

"I'm right here," he said. "And we can both throw a punch."

"Might even be fun," I added. "Like a training session." I broke away from Whistler before I lost the ability to do so, then nodded. He nodded back, and I followed him to the golden door.

Carefully, he pulled it open. We stood quietly for a few seconds, but heard nothing. We turned on our flashlights, but even they just lit the cobbled limestone path we'd walk on.

"At least the path's a little wider," I said.

Whistler zipped the guidebook up into my backpack, then wrapped his arm around my shoulders. Shaking, I wrapped my arm around his waist and then we followed the flashlight beams into the second pyramid.

I gasped. Behind us, the door had shut so fast it smacked my heel, like a shark clamping its teeth to keep its prey from escaping.

"Just keep walking," Whistler whispered. "Get out of here fast. That's our goal."

"Okay," was all I could manage. The light from my flashlight quivered with my trembling hand. Whistler squeezed my shoulder, and we quickened our pace.

"I don't see anything yet," I said.

"Just don't drop your guard. Remember defense training."

We walked like that for a minute or two, the passage changeless. I noticed gold patches on the walls. Not a gold glow or solid gold like the previous passage, but textured gold with designs.

I shone my flashlight on a wall and gasped. Instead of paintings, there were sculpted faces. The sarcophaguses were embedded in the walls.

"Don't wake up," I pleaded in a whisper, my fingers digging into Whistler's side.

We picked up our pace even more, but didn't run for fear of making too much noise. Whistler kept his arm around my shoulders and his eyes ahead, appearing determined to make it out unscathed.

I stumbled over something in the floor. Something that creaked.

Not wanting to make the mistake of pausing to see if anything was going to happen like a victim in a horror movie, I let go of Whistler and then broke into a jog. He grabbed my hand and pulled me behind him in a sprint as the walls gradually creaked as if awakening from a long sleep.

As we followed a curve to the left, a stretch of floor swung open, knocking Whistler against the wall and sending my flashlight out of my hand. When I scrambled to pick it up, a cold hand wrapped in cloth grabbed my wrist, and I screamed and stomped on it, leaving the flashlight behind.

Whistler's warm hand grabbed my own, and we bolted side by side down the path as sarcophaguses opened and creaked and mummies crawled out of the floor, ceiling and walls.

It wasn't until I'd gotten good looks at a few we'd dodged, rising in our paths, that I had hope for escaping. By themselves, they were stereotypical, save for the ornate jewelry and clothing that peeked through their bandages. They carried a burden similar to Jacob Marley and his chains in *A Christmas Carol*—their own sarcophaguses.

They wore them like clams wore shells, as protection, I assumed. *These aren't the actual mummies. Why would an artifact—an alternate artifact—need protection? Post World is supposed to be a sort of vault or safe haven for them.*

Whistler bashed the opening sarcophaguses in the walls with his flashlight as we ran, and I jumped on the ones in the floor.

"Don't let them out!" he shouted. "Remember their powers!"

I was so busy paying attention to keeping the sarcophaguses in the floor from opening that I forgot about the ones to my left. A lid slammed open in front of me, breaking Whistler's grip on my hand. And when a mummy yanked me into its lightless home, I knew that the lavish shells they carried weren't for protection, after all.

I didn't know I was screaming until the lid sealed behind me. Pressed against the withered bandaged body, I could do nothing but thrash and bang against its chest. And scream. And scream.

Above my own wailing, I thought I heard Whistler's voice from somewhere in the passage. The mummy made no sound, or it wasn't loud enough for me to hear. I felt its cool breaths on my face and its hands closing around my throat until I couldn't scream anymore. Once it thought I was almost dead, it clawed at my flesh, searching for the easiest way to open my throat or face or guts, the fastest way to make me bleed.

I cried out as it tried to drill into my collarbone, but before any blood could drizzle, the lid opened and I fell backward, against something, screaming as arms clutched my waist.

"Selk, it's me. Let's go!"

Instead of blood, tears of relief ran down my face as Whistler reclaimed my hand and pulled me along the passage, his bouncing flashlight distorting our surroundings.

As we made a right turn, the floor and walls turned to solid limestone. Whistler and I gasped for air at this point, but despite how fast we ran, the mummies still chased us.

Once my limbs stiffened, I blurted, even though I knew what was happening, "Whistler, what's...hap..." My words came out in slow echoes, as slowly as we now ran. I nearly choked as I attempted to swallow, the saliva lazy in my esophagus.

When we followed a curve to the left, our speed returned to normal, but we soon skidded to a stop at a stomach-churning roadblock ahead—two standing sarcophaguses, its residents awakening. Behind us, more mummies and sarcophaguses grew nearer, following the curve we'd just taken.

"Body shot before they wake up," I whispered to Whistler.

"Then a hook before they can even blink," he added.

Letting go of Whistler's hand, I took the mummy on the left, leaving him with the other, and threw the fastest punches I'd probably ever thrown. Whistler knocked his bandaged opponent, sarcophagus and all, down on the second blow, but I had to back up and add a front kick to the chest before mine crashed to the floor.

We slammed the lids closed and scrambled over them, then dodged a lone mummy and sarcophagus falling from the high ceiling. As Whistler, a few steps ahead of me, reached back for my hand, another lid opened, and a mummy rose from the floor.

"Whistler, watch out!"

As he looked ahead, the sitting mummy grabbed his shins, taking him down. The flashlight spiraled out of his hand and landed on the floor somewhere behind us. Its dull beam was just bright enough to reveal a door-less wall several yards ahead.

"Selk, go!"

"No!"

"Selk!"

I glanced behind me and saw the shadows of the approaching mummies with their dungeon-like shells, then looked back to Whistler. He muttered in frustration as he swung at the mummy and tried to kick free, but without his footing, he couldn't get the right angle. The mummy's sharp fingers dug into his leg, and he cried out and shouted something at it.

Now I wasn't so scared anymore. These things were really starting to tick me off.

The mummy having turned around in its sarcophagus, I lunged forward, grabbed its neck, and twisted its head to face me before hammering my knee into its eyes. The darn thing screamed and still wriggled, but at least I'd stunned it enough to free Whistler.

He limped at first as we ran, drops of blood from his leg glistening in our wake. "Almost there," I said, panting. "Almost there..."

A few yards away, my limbs stiffened again, the breath slowing in my throat. Shadows passed us on the walls as mummies approached our backs.

"Selk...Selk...Selk," Whistler's voice echoed, each repetition lasting several seconds. "The...the...the...floor...floor...floor..."

I didn't know what he meant, and I didn't have time to ask. Despite our sluggish pace, we were almost at the wall.

A strand of my hair glided into my face for a couple seconds, obscuring my vision. Once I could see again, Whistler was falling feet first to the ground as if he'd just jumped, his heel angled toward a raised limestone brick in the floor.

"Follow…follow…follow…" he said, even his waving hair sluggish in the air as he landed on and then opened a trap door.

He spun, gradually, in midair as he descended, catching my gaze and reaching for my hand as a mummy grabbed the strap of my backpack. Like struggling against gale-force winds, I pushed my hand forward and grabbed for his, but he had fallen too far.

"Whistler…Whistler…Whistler…" my voice echoed as the mummy's grip pulled me back, my feet lifting into the air and staying there several seconds. From below, Whistler cried out my name, the word echoing at first, then returning to his normal speech.

My own screams still echoed as the trap door bounced back up like a boomerang.

A foot away from the hole, I thought fast and pushed myself up and out of my backpack. A mummy's cool breath grazed my neck as I did Whistler's previous slow-motion jump and landed on the trap door with my heel. To my relief, it gave, and I caught a mummy's angry gaze before it closed as I whirled and fell, my kicking legs slow and fluid as if I were treading water in the air.

The area I fell into was dark, but not from a lack of light. The soft gold glow was back, illuminating glossy black walls like obsidian or onyx.

About halfway from the floor, the stiffness left my limbs, and it was as if I fell against the air rather than with it. The ceiling there was lower than the one on the upper level, but I still slammed into the ground.

After rolling to a stop, I lay stunned on my back, the trapdoor rattling above me. Luckily, the mummies didn't seem to have the agility to open it. "Whist…Whistler…" I murmured, pain jetting through my neck as I looked for him.

Footsteps approached, followed by my name being called. Several footsteps, several voices. Whistler reached me first and lifted me just enough to take me into his arms. I was too relieved to sob, so I just held him until Cliff and Sheridan reached us.

"We thought we'd lost you guys," Sheridan said, sounding equally relieved.

"Are you okay?" Cliff asked, crouching beside me. "We heard crashing sounds above us. What happened?"

"Congratulations, Cliff," I said, wincing as I sat up. "You and Sheridan dodged the mummies."

"And the amulet thief didn't run down your passage, after all," Whistler added, filling Cliff and Sheridan in on the arrows.

As we waited for them to contemplate the new information, I glanced at the bloody hem of Whistler's jeans. "How's your leg?"

"I've had way worse," he said. "It'll probably heal the moment I fall asleep tonight, or whenever we stop to rest. How's your head?"

"Still there."

"Can you stand?" Cliff asked, taking my arm.

"I think so."

As he and Whistler helped me up, the glossy walls blurred and twisted for a moment. Despite feeling tossed around and achy, I was fine. Yet, I still felt sick. The mummies had my backpack.

"I'm sorry, guys. I lost the guidebook."

"And I nearly lost you," Whistler murmured. "Don't worry about it. It hasn't been much help, anyway."

"It helped us figure out the arrows," I said. The trap door above us rattled again, startling me. "We can talk more later. Right now, I just want to get to the Great Pyramid of Khufu. I'm sure we'll know when we get there, even without the guidebook."

Sheridan glanced at the walls, studying some gold drawings ahead. "I don't think we're far," he said, pointing at a trace of red pigment. Not an arrow, but I got the message.

"This thief wants to be found," I said.

"We may have a guide through Post World, after all," Cliff said.

"Or just someone following orders from Fadila," I muttered.

"Regardless, let's focus on not getting separated again."

Cliff narrowed his eyes at Whistler before heading down the passage.

Sheridan shrugged before following. My heart was just starting to slow from the mummy chase. Taking a deep breath to steady myself, I set off behind them, the walking calming me further.

The passage even wider down there, Whistler came up beside me and wrapped an arm around my waist, and I leaned my head against his shoulder. All I wanted was to be back in Snow Hill, asleep in my bed with Tut purring by my feet. Maybe we'd find a safe enough place to rest here, but that didn't guarantee sleep, not after what we'd just been through. Not knowing what we still had to go through.

I hope the mummies can't follow us.

CHAPTER EIGHT

Over Years

The passage led us to this monstrous round room where the gold glow was the brightest it'd been so far, rising as tall as grass by the single curved wall. The whole area was open, save for a little section of limestone that stretched in front of the passage to, we presumed, Khufu. And despite the glow and barrenness, this was the first time I felt as if I were back on Earth in a real pyramid.

With no new threats we were aware of, we all sat and drank some water, Whistler lending me a bottle from his backpack. "At least it's not stifling in here," I said. "I heard the real pyramids can be hard to breathe in."

We sat in silence for a while before Cliff spoke. "I think now's a good time to get some sleep, but we should take shifts."

"I'll go first," I offered. "I'm too wound up to sleep."

"You need to rest, Selk," Cliff protested. "You've gotten pretty banged up since we've been here."

"Yeah, including a head injury from a falling plate." I rubbed my face, remembering the blow. "I probably need to make sure I don't have a concussion first."

"I'll stay up with you," Whistler said. "I don't think I can sleep right now either."

"But your leg needs to heal."

"At least I've got the option. You don't."

Too drained to argue further, I smiled at him. "Well, I'm glad for the company."

Cliff hesitated for a moment, but then Sheridan pulled him to the other side of the room.

I shook my head. "I've never felt so much like the floor has been pulled out from under me, like I don't know what's happening or why."

"I know what you mean," Whistler said. "It sucks feeling like that."

I met his gaze. "At least I have you to help me make some sense of it. You've been like a lifeboat in open sea."

Whistler laughed dryly. "Selk, I don't know why you keep saying stuff like that. I haven't done anything."

"You've done everything," I said, hoping he'd catch the finality in my voice.

I thought he blushed a little, probably the most vulnerable I'd ever seen him. He finally said, "I never thought doing everything would be so easy."

I blinked hard, fighting off sleep that was starting to sneak up, after all. "You haven't known me long enough. Cliff says I'm a handful."

It sounded as if he muttered, "Cliff can't even handle his own emotions," but I wasn't sure.

"What was that?" I pressed.

"Nothing."

Starting to regret volunteering for the first shift, I snuggled up to Whistler and told myself I'd just rest my head, that my eyes wouldn't close.

I couldn't see. Could barely breathe. Multiple sharp points pressed into my skin. My own screams hurt my throat. No matter how hard I fought, I couldn't get away. I heard Whistler's voice, but he was too far. He couldn't reach me. I couldn't free myself to reach him. I'd die before I got the chance to tell him that he wasn't just a crush, that I loved him so, so much.

At that fear, somehow, I was able to break free.

I bolted upright with a final scream that morphed to gasps. The first thing I saw was Cliff and Sheridan stirring on the other side of the long, round room. The second was Whistler's eyes after he tilted my chin to look at him.

"Selk?"

I took a couple seconds to catch my breath before replying, averting my eyes and running my fingers through my hair. "Sorry. I fell asleep."

"Don't apologize," he said. "I fell asleep too. You okay?"

I nodded, exhale tremblingly. "Yeah. Just a bad dream. Can't get away from the mummies, after all. I'm definitely not specializing in them if I ever get into an Egyptology program."

I tried to focus on the wall, the golden glow at its base, even Cliff and Sheridan, but the nightmare—the memory—kept harassing me. Not even a deep breath stopped the shaking.

"Mummies and claustrophobia," I added. "Not typical fears to get at the same time."

"Come here," Whistler said, then wrapped his arms around me, held me close.

I'd been so independent my whole life, I never knew just how necessary another pair of arms could be. I clung to him and sniffled once, but refused to cry over getting too close to a bandaged corpse.

Safeness enveloping me like an extra embrace, my mind went over the other part of my dream. Had I really thought that when I'd been trapped with the mummy in the sarcophagus? I'd become aware that my feelings for Whistler had grown rapidly over the past few days, but the new word alarmed me. Did I really love him, or had it been fear?

It only took a moment of searching my heart to answer myself.

I loved him. I loved him shallowly for his good looks, fighting skills and sultry demeanor. And I truly loved him for his understanding, lack of pride and for, I thought, I hoped, loving me.

Debating on whether or not to tell him, I pulled back and bit my lip.

"What's wrong?" he asked, cupping my jaw.

"I want to tell you something."

"What is it?"

I opened my mouth, but when no words came, I decided that maybe showing would be better than telling. At least for a little while longer.

Glancing up, I saw that Cliff had migrated halfway behind the section of limestone that partially covered the passage to Khufu. Looking back at Whistler, I filled my eyes with "I love you" and grabbed his hoodie to pull him in for a kiss. He traced his hands over my shoulders and back, and I pulled him closer, even dared to open my mouth.

I didn't hear the footsteps until they were about a yard away, and looked up just as Cliff shoved Whistler back.

I gasped, appalled. "Cliff!"

"What's your problem?" Whistler added, still sitting by me.

"A plain one," Cliff roared. "You're not good enough for her."

"At least I respect her and her ability to make her own decisions." Whistler stood, narrowing his eyes.

As I joined Whistler, he put his arm around my shoulders. Cliff glared with a severity I'd never seen in him before.

Then, he lunged.

Caught off guard, Whistler stumbled backward at the jab, and Cliff bolted forward and landed two right hooks before he could recover.

"Cliff!" I shouted, exasperated.

"Cliff, man, stop." Sheridan broke them apart for all of two seconds before Cliff charged again, Whistler reciprocating this time until he landed a punch that knocked Cliff against the wall. Cliff tried to retaliate, but Sheridan held him back.

Instead, he shouted, "It's not right."

"You're too old for her," Whistler retorted.

Cliff broke away from Sheridan, his eyes narrowing. "What are you talking about?"

Whistler's gaze was steady. "You've been in love with Selk for years, and it was torture already just knowing how wrong it was. Now another guy is in the picture, a guy you hate, and you don't know how to handle it. Admit it."

I expected Cliff to roll his eyes at the accusation, but he gaped at Whistler, taking me aback. What confused me even more was when Sheridan just casually arched his brow with only the faintest hint of surprise, as if he was more shocked at Whistler for calling Cliff out than by what he'd called him out on.

I returned Cliff's gape, my mind telling me this was nonsense, but my gut told me to ask. "Is that true, Cliff?"

Cliff held my gaze a long moment before answering. "Like I said, he's not good enough for you, Selk."

My eyes widened. "Because you think *you* are?"

Cliff started to speak, but then turned and walked toward the open passage.

At the risk of the group getting separated again, I ran after him, grabbing his arm when I caught up to him. "Cliff?" He stopped, but didn't turn around. "You've known me for years," I said. "Why won't you talk to me?"

At that, he faced me, but he still didn't speak, just smiled sadly for a second and reached for me. I reached back, thinking he was going to hug me and apologize and blame his acting so weird on the stress of Post World, but he did none of those three things.

Instead, he kissed me.

And it wasn't a light kiss, either. It was one that had gained interest over time. Over years.

Used to kissing Whistler, I instinctively moved my lips for a second, but alerts flashed in my mind about how disturbing this was. I reacted so quickly, I couldn't distinguish the actions. All I knew was that I'd just done some complicated self-defense maneuver that involved punching, kneeing and kicking, and that I was now standing a few feet away from a wheezing, doubled-over Cliff.

Once I realized my fingers were still curled in tense fists, I forced them to relax. "What the…" was all I could say as I stared at Cliff in shock.

He straightened after a few seconds, daring to look me in the eyes, his face fallen. "I take that as you realizing how creepy this is."

I bit my lip, contemplating his statement. "Not creepy, exactly. Mainly weird."

Cliff sighed and averted his eyes. "I'm eight years older than you, practically your big brother. Of course it's weird." He hesitated a moment, then looked back up and took a step toward me. "I know it's wrong, but you've always felt right for me."

Shaking my head, I turned away. "Never saw it coming. I don't know what to say."

"I was going to tell you, either on your birthday or after graduation. Then *he* showed up."

Meeting his gaze, I said, "Cliff, you're right." When he looked at me expectantly, I wanted to throw up. "This is creepy."

His face fell, but he nodded. "Yeah. I know. He's only got three or four years on you. That's a lot better than eight. At your age, at least."

I sighed, running a hand through my hair. "And of all times, you tell me *now*? In another dimension?"

His eyes narrowed. "I hadn't planned on it. He told you for me."

Trying to choose my words carefully, I said, "Cliff. You're really special to me, but…" Taking a deep breath, I admitted, "I am in love with Whistler.

He gives me butterflies. I've never had butterflies before."

It was as if the mummies had come back, turning everything to slow motion. Cliff looked both guilty and crushed. He stood with that pain in his eyes for the longest moment before turning to walk farther down the passage.

"Tell them to keep up," he muttered. "We need to get moving."

Dazed, I jogged back to the others to relay the message. Cliff was really in love with me, and I still couldn't believe it, even after seeing his heart in his eyes.

"What happened?" Whistler asked.

"You didn't see?"

He shook his head. "Couldn't look. We don't have time for another brawl."

I was about to reply, but then I saw the sheepish look on Sheridan's face. "You knew, didn't you?"

"Yeah," he admitted. "Even I thought it was creepy."

Whistler's irritated expression softened. "It's got to hurt to lose you. I feel bad for the guy." He cupped my jaw. "I won't ever lose you, will I?"

"No," I replied without hesitation.

We caught up to Cliff in silence, and not wanting to torture him, I held Whistler's hand for a moment before dropping it, as if we were walking out of the alley in Snow Hill again.

* * * *

It took me a while to realize the high ceiling lowered the farther we walked. No one commented until the guys had to duck.

"I'm starting to feel like peanut butter in a sandwich," Sheridan said, stooping even lower as he progressed.

"Stupid mummies," I muttered. "That guidebook would be very nice right about now."

The passage had widened, at least enough for all of us to crawl side by side. Being the shortest, I was the last to sink to my hands and knees. The roof didn't stop sloping, and when we were flat against the floor, the guys having had to take off their backpacks, we halted.

"Maybe we took a wrong turn," Cliff muttered.

I was glad he was beside the left wall with Sheridan and Whistler between us. Even separated, I winced at the awkwardness. Of all the things to regret right now, I wished I'd have spent more time doing girl stuff with Brandie and Lynette instead of hanging out with guys at the gym all day. I didn't want to picture their faces when or if they found out how Cliff felt about me. Things before Egypt had been so much easier. In just a couple days, I'd grown up more than I'd realized.

Moving his hair away from his forehead, Whistler closed his original eyes and squinted with his third at the path ahead of us. "Maybe we didn't. There's a square tunnel up ahead, but..." He squinted again.

"What is it?" I pressed.

"It's a straight drop, and I can't see where it ends."

"It's pitch black," Sheridan confirmed.

My breath caught, but I forced myself not to panic. The mummies were gone. All we had to do was make it out of Khufu to Ramses III's palace and then it'd be easier to navigate—until we got to the labyrinth.

"I'll check it out," Whistler volunteered. "You guys stay here."

"Wait," I said, grabbing his arm. "We don't know where it goes or what's down there. Let's think about this for a little while."

He smiled at me and squeezed my hand. "It'll be no time. I'll bring a flashlight so Sheridan and Cliff can get a better look at the tunnel."

I bit my lip, hesitating. "Maybe I should go. You might be too broad-shouldered to fit."

"It's wide enough," he protested.

After a bit more hesitation, I gave him a quick kiss—not caring about Cliff being there—and said, "Be careful." In a whisper, I added, "Losing you would hurt too."

We all crawled to the edge of the dark tunnel. Whistler got a flashlight and rope out of his backpack. "I probably won't need this, but just in case," he said, tying the rope to a large protruding brick in the floor.

I tied the end around his waist. "And just in case the tunnel is longer than expected."

"Don't worry, man," Sheridan said. "We've got your back." He glanced at Cliff. "I have, at least."

"So have I," Cliff forced.

Whistler met my gaze before lowering himself into the tunnel, not even holding onto the rope once there. Pressing his shoes against one wall and his back against the opposite, he made sure he had a good grip before beginning his descent.

I bit my lip, not believing how worried I was. He'd gotten beaten up plenty of times in Snow Hill, but not by mummies or crocodiles or who knew what else.

"Looks good so far," he said, interrupting my thoughts. "And I can actually see the bottom now. It's not as deep as I thought."

"I can see it too," Sheridan confirmed. "What's that shadow in the middle?"

"Shadow?" I repeated, swallowing hard.

"I don't know," Whistler called, his voice fainter, echoing, reminding me of the mummy chase. "I'm having trouble angling the flashlight."

"Looks like a big rock," Sheridan said, his third eye squinting. "It doesn't seem like it's going to jump up or anything."

None of us said anything else as we waited for Whistler to reach the bottom of the tunnel.

Finally, I heard his voice significantly farther away. "Coast is clear." He added, "Selk, you're not going to believe this!"

"What?" I called.

"It's hard to hear you," he replied. "Come down and see."

He tugged on the rope to let us know he'd untied himself, but I stopped Sheridan from pulling it back up. "I'll just hold on to it. Doesn't sound too hard to walk to the bottom."

"Selk—"

"You never know when you may have to pull both of us up," I said, cutting Cliff off before he could protest. "Whoever goes last, throw the backpacks down. I'll tell Whistler to step out of the way."

Gripping the rope, I lowered myself into the tunnel. Most people are advised to not look down in such situations, but looking down at Whistler's flashlight was the only thing keeping me from panicking. I just wanted to get it over with as fast as I could.

Once I saw I was only a few feet from the bottom, I jumped to the floor, stumbling a little on the new slick surface. Whistler took my arm to steady me, the expression on his face unreadable.

"What's wrong?" I asked, glancing around warily.

"I think you just broke the record for the fastest rappel into a tunnel."

I grinned, relieved, and tugged on the rope to let Cliff and Sheridan know I was at the bottom. "It was pretty fun." Now that I was out of the small, dark space. Glancing up, it seemed a lot farther.

Whistler smiled. "You're amazing."

I kept his gaze for a moment, then said, "We need to move away from the tunnel. I told them whoever goes last needs to throw the backpacks down."

"Speaking of which," Whistler began, "look what was waiting for us."

I hadn't seen it before because the only light down there was Whistler's flashlight. Now, as he picked it up, I was both ecstatic and terrified. Ecstatic, because I had it back. Terrified, because I knew what had brought it there.

"My backpack," I said. "Did you take the guidebook out?"

"No," he said. "I found it like that, the guidebook propped up against it."

After slipping my backpack on, I clutched the guidebook in both hands, whispering, "And you're sure we're alone down here?"

Whistler wrapped an arm around my shoulders and pointed at the top of the guidebook with his flashlight. "No mummies, but I wouldn't say we're entirely alone."

Looking closer, I saw the familiar red chalk smudged in the shape of fingerprints. "The thief," I said. "Maybe he or she really is trying to help."

"You guys still down there?" Sheridan called, not too far above us. "I can't see anything even with three eyes."

"Sorry," Whistler replied, then shone his flashlight toward the tunnel.

A few seconds later, Sheridan jumped down as I'd done, but apparently, he'd jumped from too high up, because he fell on the slick onyx-like floor.

"How'd you guys get down here so fast?" he wondered aloud as he rose to his feet, then tugged the rope. A few seconds later, the guys' backpacks fell to the bottom of the tunnel, and Sheridan and Whistler slipped theirs on.

I told the two guys about the guidebook after Cliff came down, then flipped through it to make sure the amulet thief hadn't written any clues inside. Nothing new, but I did notice something I hadn't before—the last page was written in English, the tone like a diary entry.

After scanning it, I summarized for the guys. "So apparently what we've encountered so far was nothing compared to what'll happen when or if we finally return the amulet. Zahid must have written this the last time he was here."

"Does it give any details?" Sheridan asked.

"'After *Ummi* returned the jar,'" I quoted, "'almost all of Post World came together, to welcome the artifact home, I suppose. That welcome was what killed Qubilah.' There aren't any other details. The rest just talks about how Fadila, Naim and Zahid barely escaped, and how distraught they were over my aunt's death."

"So they actually saw her die," Whistler said. "That means she couldn't be the one who took the amulet."

"I just have no clue who else could have taken it," I said.

"Only one way to find out," Cliff muttered, the first thing he'd said since before coming down the tunnel.

After grabbing a flashlight out of his backpack, he shone it around the small, dark area before finding another passageway. Another small one with no gold light in sight.

Whistler wound up the rope and then zipped it into his backpack before following Cliff. Sheridan followed Whistler. I yet again stopped myself from having a panic attack.

Leaning against the wall, I took a deep breath. I'd just freaking rappelled down a dark tunnel, and I couldn't merely crawl through another one?

No, I could. I had to.

Cliff disappeared with his flashlight into the new claustrophobia inducer, but Sheridan and Whistler lingered.

"Cliff, man, wait a second," Sheridan said, studying me. "You all right, honey?"

Whistler must have seen the fear on my face, because he frowned and walked to me. "You okay?" he asked, placing his hands on my shoulders.

I nodded, taking another deep breath. "Yeah. Just give me a… Yeah."

I grabbed his hand and pulled him behind me, unable to meet his gaze.

The tunnel. That was all I needed to focus on right now, getting through it, and then I'd be all right.

After reluctantly letting go of his hand, I grabbed a flashlight from my backpack, dropped to my hands and knees and plunged past Sheridan into the onyx tunnel. For such an extravagant history, the alternate version of ancient Egypt could be pretty monotonous.

Soon I caught up to Cliff and became frustrated when he wasn't moving fast enough. *No walls are going to close. The guys are in here with you. We're all going to get out. Everything is fine.*

It seemed as if we'd made a trillion turns before Whistler called from the back, "There's gold light up ahead. It shouldn't be too much longer, Selk."

I squinted at Cliff, but his flashlight blurred everything ahead.

"Um…" Sheridan began. "Actually…"

"What is it, Sheridan?" I asked.

"There's something weird ahead," Cliff said. "A shadow or something."

Before I could imagine too many bone-crushing mummies, Whistler said, "The thief! Speed up, Cliff."

"Shut your mouth!" Cliff hissed. "We need to sneak up."

Whistler muttered something that sounded like, "I'll show you 'sneaking up.'"

Relieved we were doing the chasing rather than being chased, I punched Cliff's calf to tell him Whistler had the right idea.

Luckily, the tunnel ended soon, so we could switch places. Though the guys had paranormal powers, I felt I could have outrun any of them.

The new room hindered my plan. It was shaped like a pyramid, but it was hard to tell whether or not the roof ended in a point, because the walls, floor and ceiling were all made out of jade. The walls were like giant bubble-wrap. Even though the gold glow was bright, the room was so abstract I couldn't even see the passage we'd just come from.

Turning to the guidebook, I flipped pages until I found the last page on Khufu, because I assumed we were approaching the last pyramid's end. The first paragraph was in Arabic, but the second was in a language I didn't recognize—at first. I gasped, clamping a hand over my mouth.

"What is it, Selk?" Whistler asked.

"The second half of the page is in Croatian." I stopped a tear from falling. "I can't read Croatian. The only word I recognize is my name. My grandpa must have absorbed some power to help return an artifact before or right after I was born." *I'm sorry. I forgive you.*

Cliff's face softened, and he stepped forward as if about to put his arm around me. He stopped and averted his eyes after glancing at Whistler, the new, awkward Cliff returning.

Knowing Whistler's arms would only make me cry, I avoided his gaze and mumbled, "I can't believe I'm part Croatian and can't speak a word."

"I speak a little Croatian."

I looked at Sheridan. "Seriously?"

"Yeah. I trained some triplets from Croatia, who moved to the States for some new competition. They didn't know much English, so I took an online class."

"Why didn't you ever tell me?" I asked in disbelief.

"I didn't think about it," he said.

I laughed and handed him the guidebook. "Can you translate this?"

"I can't read everything," he said, "but I think it says something about..." He furrowed his brows. "No, that can't be right. Maybe I don't remember Croatian, after all."

"What does it say, Sheridan?" I pressed.

"Something about squeezing toothpaste up a drain and hugging a gold floor."

"*Up* a drain?" Whistler repeated.

"Toothpaste?" I added.

Sheridan shrugged. "Like I said, I must have forgotten what I learned."

I shifted to look around the room. Taken aback when I bumped into a wall, I glanced at the guys. They seemed closer to the walls than they'd been a few seconds ago.

"Guys," I said, "take a couple steps toward me."

After they did, I stood still and watched for a few seconds. It happened so gradually I almost missed it, but when I closed my eyes for a moment and reopened them, I saw it. The guys were right beside the wall again. And they hadn't moved.

"Sheridan," I breathed, "your Croatian isn't as bad as you'd thought.

My grandpa had to have gotten out of this somehow because he wrote it down, but he was talking about the room. The room squeezed him like toothpaste!" I stumbled forward when the wall crept up behind me. What else would worsen my claustrophobia?

Sheridan glanced at the roof. "The guidebook said 'up a drain.'"

I followed his gaze. The ceiling had shifted, revealing more gold light. "'Hugging a gold floor!'"

"The floor is pushing us toward the roof," Whistler said.

I looked at the walls, and they looked shorter than they had when we'd first gotten there. He was right. The walls and floors must have been taking turns, the floor gradually breaking off.

"Sheridan," I said, "you're the strongest. We'll wait until the floor is almost to the ceiling and give you a leg up so you can help pull us out."

"It'll be too late by then," Cliff said. "We'll lift you and then follow."

"No!" I shouted, panicking now. "I can't lift you guys!" There was barely any room around us now, and the floor still wasn't close enough to the ceiling to climb through.

"If we time it right," Whistler said, "we can all make it." Closing his eyes, he shoved his hair off his forehead and aimed his third eye at the roof. He took the rope out of his backpack and then tied a lasso.

"What are you doing?" I asked.

"Getting us out of here," he said. "Sheridan, can I borrow your shoulders?"

Sheridan nodded and knelt, but looked at him questioningly.

With one hand against the closing wall for balance, Whistler stepped onto Sheridan's shoulders and stood straight. "Okay," he said.

Sheridan rose to his full height, his muscles appearing unaffected by the weight. Whistler could almost touch the ceiling, the point having widened a bit more.

Still using his third eye, he tossed the rope over and over again before it caught something. Without pausing, he left Sheridan's shoulders and used it to climb up the slick jade wall.

I gasped when it pushed me into Sheridan, not realizing how small the room had gotten. As I looked back up, Whistler crawled into the ceiling, which was only a few feet away now. A second later, the rope fell.

"Selk, grab the rope!" Whistler called.

Sheridan and Cliff grabbed me by the knees and lifted me so I wouldn't have far to climb. I swallowed hard as I neared the top, the walls pressing into my shoulders. We had to get Cliff and Sheridan out.

Once I emerged, I squinted at the increased brightness, but didn't have time to take in the new surroundings. Whistler helped me onto solid ground before returning his attention to the others. We both stood and grabbed the rope, pulling until Cliff crawled into the gold light, but he'd barely managed to squeeze through.

"Sheridan, hurry!" I screamed, all three of us pulling as hard as we could. His shoulders made it before he got stuck.

"Lose your backpack, man!" Cliff shouted.

Sheridan ducked below the ceiling, which had stopped opening, and a moment later, yelled, "Okay, guys, pull!" After several moments of using all our strength, he finally crawled onto the ground, the ceiling closing and disappearing in his wake.

"The 'hugging a gold floor' part makes sense now," he said, panting, his arms spread wide across the glow.

Breathing a sigh of relief, I collapsed beside Sheridan, and said, "Fast thinking, Whistler."

Whistler fell next to me, and Cliff sat a few feet away, nothing but gold light for a ground and darker gold light for a sky. And for a moment, I missed him. The old Cliff, before he'd startled me with that secret.

Not caring we weren't alone, I sat up, and said, "You know, Cliff, I'm not always an all-or-nothing kind of girl, and you don't have to be an all-or-nothing guy. I miss you."

He met my gaze, his eyes widening at my change of subject. "I miss *you*," he admitted. "Nothing can compete with a new requited romance."

Regretting bringing the subject up, I averted my eyes and didn't say anything else.

After a few moments, Sheridan spoke. "On a brighter note, I may have had to lose my backpack, but..." He reached into his shirt. "I have the guidebook."

"You keep amazing me," I said, grinning as he handed it to me. He shrugged and smirked.

I studied the beginning of the palace's map. It was blank, save for three triangles and what appeared to be a palace with columns. Looking ahead, I saw nothing but the gold light. I knew which direction to go.

Standing, I said, "We're almost to the palace. It's by the pyramidia of the pyramids we just went through."

"Pyramidia?" Sheridan repeated.

"The tops of pyramids," I said. "At least that's what I assume. And if I'm right, the three pyramids are almost completely buried in this gold ground." Ahead, the gold shimmered a little. "Did you guys see that?"

"See what?" Whistler asked.

After studying the spot for a moment, I shook my head. "Never mind. My eyes are playing tricks on me."

Whistler took the rope off the large brick he'd lassoed, then we all set off into the changeless gold light. *The surroundings are certainly appropriate for a palace.* As we walked, my stomach tensed. We still had two places to navigate, and we hadn't even seen the crocodiles yet.

Still, I doubted there was anything there worse than mummies.

CHAPTER 9

Famous Youth

I wondered if the concept of reality had vanished when the unremitting gold void, like a cool, bright desert, changed in the slightest.

"The pyramidia," I said, exhaling in relief at the sight of the three sharp hills a little way off. I was so happy to see them, I would have run to them if I hadn't been physically and emotionally exhausted.

They appeared to be just taller than Sheridan, and about twenty meters separated each of them. About fifty meters off, an ivory structure that glittered like drusy stood as tall as it was wide. In this strange world, pyramids were almost insignificant compared to the palace.

"Now leaving Khufu," I commented, taking in the impressive palace. "Selket must have had a full-time job, guarding both interiors and exteriors."

"What does the guidebook say about this place?" Whistler asked.

Before I could take it out of my backpack, the gold shimmered ahead as it'd done earlier, this time harshly.

"Did you guys see that?" I asked.

"Yeah," Sheridan said. "It almost looked like a figure."

I stared at the same spot until it shimmered again, a little to the right. It took a few moments to recognize the movement.

"The thief is running!" I said. My adrenaline back, I sprinted, the guys right behind me.

"He's heading for the palace," Cliff said. "Maybe we can corner him there."

We reached the massive staircase just as the thief disappeared behind one of the broad columns, the ivory glittering even more up close in the gold light.

Without pausing for breath, I started up the stairs, taking them two at a time. Though the thief was nowhere in sight, I kept running once at the top, and was surprised to find that, inside, the palace was devoid of any décor or artifacts. There was nothing but countless wide columns and a floor and roof made of the same glittering ivory. That must have meant that Selket hadn't guarded treasures of the palace, but the palace itself, or maybe its inhabitants.

My exhaustion overwhelming my adrenaline, the guys passed me, but I kept going. Another flash of gold wove between three columns ahead just before the whole palace shuddered, throwing me off balance.

As I regained my footing, there was a noise like concrete scraping together. To my left, a little way ahead, a column wriggled, then kicked away from the floor and then swung in a wide circle.

"Guys, look out!" I managed to scream in between panting.

The guys turned toward me before noticing the column. They ran in my direction, but I couldn't understand what they shouted, because their voices collided.

When I heard the scraping behind me, I realized what they said and picked up my speed, but I'd underestimated how tall the columns were, how far they could reach. A blow to my side knocked me several yards to the left and into a still column. Before I could fall, a second one nearby scraped against the one I leaned on, the blow to my head sending me rolling across the floor. A scream of pain tried to escape, but it took everything I had just to breathe.

The guys kept shouting as they approached. It took them a long time with every new column that kicked away from the floor. Lying stunned on my backpack, out of my peripheral vision, I saw a figure dodge a swinging column and lie down as well.

Whistler must have seen him too, because he shouted something at the guys before dropping to his hands and knees and crawling as low to the floor as he could. The guys mimicked him as the figure to my left edged away and out of sight, the swinging columns four or five feet above the ground.

Almost all the columns swung now, and I feared the roof would collapse with so few to hold it up, but this was Post World, not Earth. For all I knew, the roof could float on its own.

Something warm rolling onto my nose pushed my fears of the roof holding away. I wanted to see if I could stand, but I couldn't with the columns still circling. My ears ringing, I tried to estimate how badly I was hurt by where and how intense the pain was—pain was everywhere, and it was strong.

The backpack not helping, I managed to roll onto my side with a groan as the guys reached me, Whistler first. Unable to sit up because of the columns, he shifted onto his side to face me and pulled the backpack straps over my arms.

"Selk," he said, barely above a whisper.

"I'll be fine," I managed. "We just need to get out of here."

Cliff reached me next. "Selk," he said, his previous stony face softening, "are you okay?"

As I tasted blood, I tensed, fearing it was coming from the inside, but I remembered the stream trickling down my face. Wiping my mouth, I said, "Yeah," though I still wasn't sure.

Too difficult to reach into a backpack at the moment, Whistler used his hoodie for a towel and wiped the blood off my face.

"What should we do?" Sheridan asked. "Do you guys think this place is going to come down? Should we—"

A fierce shudder cut him off. We all rolled onto our backs (Cliff and Whistler onto their backpacks) to avoid the unsettled columns, which dipped low at the movement.

The shuddering didn't stop. The palace tilted like a spinning top. Whistler wrapped his arms around me to keep me from sliding away, but Cliff and Sheridan were pushed several feet.

Glancing to my right, over Whistler's chest, I saw the source of the new commotion. The outside columns, and who knew what other ones, were awakening, throwing the palace off balance.

Just when I thought the roof would finally cave in, the wobbling stopped, and the palace leveled out. The columns overhead still spun, but closer to the entrance now. When I saw the ones outside, I realized there was actually a purpose for this chaos.

"Besides the temple," I said, "the palace is the easiest place to go through." Whistler looked at me as if I'd lost my mind, but I elaborated before he could comment. "The columns," I said. "The ones in here act like a crank, and the ones outside…" I jerked my chin toward the entrance, the outside columns rising, lifting the palace. After Whistler followed my gaze, realization dawned on his face.

"It's like an elevator," he said. "So all we really had to do here was lie on the floor until the palace rose."

"The thief has to still be in here," I said. "Whoever it is knows what's happening, because I saw a figure lie down beneath the columns."

Whistler's eyes widened.

"What is it?" I asked.

Turning away, he called, but not too loudly, "Cliff, Sheridan, can you crawl toward the back of the palace?"

"Why?" Cliff asked.

Whistler muttered under his breath, losing his patience. "The thief is still in here. We need to corner him before the palace stops rising."

As Cliff and Sheridan crawled away, I said, "Go with them. I'll catch up."

Whistler turned back to me, searching my eyes in disbelief. "Selk, I'm not leaving you, and definitely not like this. Who knows how many of your bones could be broken."

The pain and shock of the blows starting to wear off, I protested, "I don't think I broke anything." I gasped when the palace jerked. The columns overhead slowed and began returning to their posts.

I was relieved until I realized where Whistler and I were lying. He saw the descending column at the same time and pulled us out of the way before it could press us into the milky, glittering floor.

"Ding," I whispered, mimicking the sound of an elevator stopping at another level.

We lay there a few seconds, savoring the moment of peace until it was interrupted by Cliff's and Sheridan's running footsteps.

"We couldn't find the thief," Sheridan said.

I sighed. "I expected that. Whoever it is obviously has a thorough understanding of Post World."

Cliff crouched beside me. "Can you stand, Selk?"

Whistler helped me sit up. When no significant pain shot through my ribs or other important bones, he and Cliff took either of my arms and helped me to my feet. I winced at the all-over achiness, and my vision blurred for a moment, but nothing felt broken. My head hurt the worst. I wiped away a fresh trickle of blood from the side of my face, and the guys added another bandage to my growing collection.

"Thanks," I said. "Are you guys okay?"

They nodded, then Whistler said, "I'm worried about your head. That's the second blow you took."

"Third time a knockout?" I blinked to clear my sporadically blurring vision. "I'm fine. Let's go." Though reaching the end of Post World didn't mean we could leave, I kept telling myself that the more progress we made, the sooner we could go home.

Free of a backpack, Sheridan offered to carry mine. We only walked a few feet toward the palace's entrance before stopping. After the commotion with the palace rising, we'd assumed we wouldn't have to walk all the way through it to reach the labyrinth, but the entrance was now blocked by a non-glowing gold wall.

For the second time in Post World, I wondered where our source of light was coming from, then glanced up. The palace's ceiling glowed now, ivory instead of gold.

We turned around and passed seemingly infinite columns as we walked through the palace.

"I never thought I'd say this," I said, "but it's nice to not be running." I couldn't have run now even if I'd wanted to. I hoped that would change. There were probably still a lot of things ahead that needed running from.

After a few more minutes of walking, the changeless palace finally led us to an elaborately decorated wide hall with a dark wooden floor and hieroglyphics covering the glittering ivory walls.

As I looked up to admire the murals on the arched roof, my vision blurred again, this time almost going out. Blood fled from my head, leaving my face and lips numb. My knees buckled.

"Selk, are you all right?" Whistler asked, catching me.

"I'm good," I said. Before I could protest further, he lifted me into his arms. "Whistler," I grumbled, "you can't carry me and your backpack. I'm fine. Just set me down and—" He interrupted my sentence with a weird look that was half admiration and half finality.

"You should have lain still a little longer," he said, walking. "It's just multitasking. We can keep moving through Post World while you recover."

"He's right," Cliff said, startling both of us. "And Sheridan and I can take shifts if he gets tired."

I rolled my eyes, though I was glad Cliff had shown a little of his old self. "That won't be necessary. I just need a second."

Whistler smiled and planted a light kiss on my lips, and we kept each other's gaze for a moment before he looked ahead. I rested my head against his collarbone, watching the path with my peripheral vision.

With my dizziness, I couldn't remember who'd had the guidebook last, but somehow Cliff had gotten it and studied it as he walked.

After a moment, he stopped, and said, "I think now might be a good time for a break." We all stopped with him.

"Why?" Sheridan asked.

"Because Selk's in no condition to wrestle crocodiles right now."

I looked at him, my eyes widening. "The venom pool? Seriously?"

Cliff nodded. "According to the map, this passage will take us right to it. And if we can get across, we'll be at the labyrinth."

I exchanged glances with Whistler. So much had been happening I hadn't realized how close we were to the venom pool. "But the thief," I said.

"Cliff's right," Whistler said. "We'll catch the thief soon enough, but we need to sit down and come up with a plan for dealing with the crocodiles first. The thief might even give us more hints."

Whistler set me against the wall before shrugging out of his backpack and then sitting next to me. Cliff and Sheridan slid down the wall across from us.

We all sat in silence for a while, the guys probably thinking about the columns we'd just avoided. So near Whistler now, I could only think about how close we'd gotten, how close we kept growing. I never would have guessed that I'd meet my dream guy in a secret club called Man Cave.

"Whistler, what's your middle name?" I added with a smile, "Besides 'The Dread Whisperer,' that is."

Whistler glanced at me, taken aback, then returned my smile. "Aric. With an 'A.'"

My head already on his shoulder, I almost leaned in to kiss him, but then I saw Cliff out of the corner of my eye, who looked as if he was about to throw up. Sheridan, on the other hand, unsuccessfully struggled to prevent a smile from breaking free. He'd gone from sympathetic to exposed, hopeless romantic in less than a day.

After a few minutes, I said, "So, the crocodiles. Did you read anything that will help us, Cliff?"

"I'm not sure," he said, only a hint of nausea lingering on his face. He opened the guidebook again. "There's something in English that says 'like a curtain of gold,' but the first part of the sentence is smudged, and even the part that isn't is hard to read. The handwriting is different than the other handwritings in the book."

"Dude, practically every room in this whole place is gold or has gold of some kind," Sheridan said. "How does that help?"

"Exactly," Cliff said.

"That does help," Whistler countered. "At least a little."

"How?" Cliff challenged. "Do you see any gold curtains around here?"

"No," Whistler admitted, "but we know it's not a gold floor or wall or roof, and definitely not a gold artifact. And the gold light isn't exactly like a curtain."

I thought back to when the column had knocked me down, how I'd seen the gold figure sneak away. "Clothing can flow like a curtain," I said. "The amulet thief is wearing gold."

"How long has the amulet thief been here?" Cliff asked. "This can't mean the thief's clothing."

"Some kind of clothing," Whistler protested. "That's the only thing that makes sense, at least in this place."

"Maybe," I said. "Now I'm really confused."

As the guys argued about what the sentence could have meant, my lids grew heavier. I'd just taken a nap not long ago, but I couldn't hold my eyes open. My last thought before I drifted off was something about not caring how dangerous it was to sleep with a head injury, let alone two.

* * * *

When I woke up, Sheridan and Cliff were arguing, but Whistler was asleep. I smiled, pulling back a little to study him. His silky hair was post-apocalyptic, strands sticking up or down or out or any random way like an explosion, and I wanted to kiss those dirty-blond eyelashes. I'd never realized how thick they were.

Cliff and Sheridan still distracted by their argument, I leaned close to Whistler and whispered against his serene face. "You're beautiful." Closing my eyes, I placed my hand on his heart. "Inside and out."

After Sheridan and Cliff stopped talking, I pretended to be asleep, but I hadn't fooled them.

"Sleep well, Selk?" Cliff asked.

As Whistler stirred beside me, I sighed and opened my eyes. "Yeah. Did you guys get any sleep?"

"Yeah, actually," Cliff said. "I lost track of the time. I'm not sure how long we've been in Post World now, whether it's night or day back in Egypt."

"Did you guys figure out anything new about the crocodiles?" Whistler asked groggily, blinking heavily.

Cliff sighed. "No."

"That one line is the only thing written next to the map of the venom pool," Sheridan said.

"How are you feeling?" Whistler asked me.

"Like I could wrestle a crocodile."

To prove my point, I stood, fighting off the little bit of dizziness that threatened me, and offered him a hand. He took it with a smile, but stood on his own.

"Let's get this over with," I said, then admitted, "I'll probably eat my words once we're actually there, but I'm kind of excited to see the labyrinth. At least Post World's version of it."

Sheridan laughed. "So we're going into this with nothing but a description of what could possibly be gold clothing and a plan to take down crocodiles with our bare hands."

I took a deep breath. "The first descendants of Selket didn't even have the description."

I grabbed a hair tie out of my pocket and slid my locks into a ponytail. I was already rebelling against head injuries. Trying to keep hair out of my face wouldn't help my concentration while taming crocodiles.

Sliding my backpack on, I said, "Let's go," and then continued down the palace hall.

"Selk, wait." Cliff rushed up beside me and put a hand on my shoulder to stop me. "It's literally right around the corner." He showed me the map, and sure enough, crocodiles lurked only a few yards away.

I gaped at him. "We slept while crocodiles are swimming in venom nearby?"

"There's something to brag to the guys about," Sheridan said a little way behind us.

Recovering, I met Cliff's familiar blue-eyed gaze. Lowering my voice so the others couldn't hear, I said, "Cliff, I don't want you to think I'm trying to flaunt my relationship with Whistler. He's just really helping me. Through everything. Not that you haven't, but…" I bit my lip, unsure of how to continue. "Whenever I hold his hand or kiss him or rest my head on his shoulder, it's not to hurt you. Just understand that."

Cliff kept my gaze a long moment before saying, "Whatever. Let's spar with some crocodiles."

He threw a small smile over his shoulder as he continued down the hall. Though he couldn't see me, I smiled back, relieved. He'd make the right girl really happy one day. I pictured him with a pretty blonde, maybe an older version of Brandie, though I'd never crush her hopes by telling her that.

The high ceiling grew lower and lower, and for a moment, I was afraid we'd have to crawl again as we'd done before rappelling down the tunnel. Thankfully, its lowest point was still a few feet above the guys' heads.

The light grew dimmer and changed from gold to green, as well as the walls, floor and ceiling. "It's all raw emerald," I said in wonder, running my hand over the translucent wall, uneven yet glossy.

We walked side by side for a while, but after turning a corner, we stopped. Everything was the same emerald texture, and the ceiling was the same height, but the room was vast, more like a lake than a pool. A pool so clear, I'd be able to see a shard of glass at the bottom.

I was certainly able to see the rich emerald scales, translucent like the walls.

There were seven crocodiles. Each was about ten feet in length without including its tail. Those were so long, they touched the bottom of the pool, a large point like a scorpion's stinger at the ends.

As the crocodiles' snakelike tongues tasted the venom they swam in, I wondered if they sensed us.

Across the pool, in the back wall, was a small door we'd probably have to duck into, maybe even crawl. I swallowed hard. How could all of us make it through quickly enough? Getting through that door depended on how many crocodiles could be tamed, and for how long they would stay tame.

A curtain of gold, a curtain of gold... I glanced around the room, but nothing stood out. Everything was green, save for the colorless venom.

As a crocodile swam close to our side of the pool, we pressed our backs against the wall to stay out of its sight. "What do we do?" I whispered. "I don't see anything gold."

"We definitely shouldn't rush into anything," Cliff said.

"We haven't seen the whole room," I protested. "What if there's something gold in one of the corners? Maybe we should get a little clo—" I froze at a rumbling sound to my far left, behind Whistler and Sheridan.

"Start moving toward the pool," Whistler said. "Slowly."

I knew what was behind us. I just didn't know why. Did the crocodiles leave their "post" in Post World? If that was the case, anything could leave its post. Even mummies. Maybe even artifacts.

"Guys," I whispered as we edged along the wall, "what if the animate artifacts can leave their post? Do you think that's what the guidebook means?"

"*Flowing* gold," Sheridan corrected, glancing nervously at the expanding shadow behind him.

My pulse quickening, I thought as hard as I could. This whole place was a puzzle, and we'd figured out everything so far. How could gold help us when there was nothing gold in sight?

As we neared the pool, I studied it hard, then slowed when I noticed something odd. At first glance, the room had appeared to be nothing but the pool with a narrow line of dry emerald floor in front of it. Closer, I noticed thinner lines in the pool, dividers.

The middle was the largest block, the one where the crocodiles swam. In narrow strips like long water troughs, one on either side of the main pool, the venom was a shade darker.

"Poison," I said, squinting. "The pool is divided into venom and poison."

"The sides are shallow too," Cliff said. "Shallow enough to wade through."

"If they weren't filled with poison," Sheridan reminded, glancing at a hissing noise behind us. "Um… Guys…"

I looked when he didn't elaborate. The crocodile was still a little way off, but it stared at us now, its speed increasing.

"Selk," Cliff said, "I think I found the flowing gold."

He pointed at the back left corner of the pool, where I could barely make out a gold dot. "I can't see as far as you guys," I said. "What is it? Is it floating in the poison?"

"No," Whistler said. "There's a small square of dry floor in each of the back corners. It's a pile of clothes, after all."

A little relief stroked my gut—at least there was something relevant about the sentence in the guidebook—but I still didn't understand how a pile of clothes could help us tame one crocodile, let alone seven.

"So, what?" I began. "We just wave them at the crocodiles like a matador with a bull?"

Whistler was about to speak, then stopped when our gazes met. He kept mine for a long moment, so long I was about to remind him that this wasn't an appropriate time for romance. As he glanced at the pile of clothes, I realized he'd gotten an idea.

"Selk, this may sound crazy, but I think I know how to tame the crocodiles." He added, "How you can tame the crocodiles."

I jumped at another hiss behind us, louder this time, accompanied by determined thumps against the floor. With no options, we bolted toward the pool and seven more crocodiles. Two of them stayed at the back of the room, hissing at something in the exit. The other five swam toward us, leisurely.

With nowhere else for us to go, Cliff whirled on Whistler. "Are you kidding? You're going to hide behind your girlfriend?"

Losing his patience, Whistler grabbed Cliff by the collar of his shirt. "If I'm right about that book, she's the only one who can get us past the crocodiles. Now, would you rather her die than save herself? Because none of us can save her this time, and if we waste time trying, she will die."

Not giving Cliff time to reply, I grabbed Whistler's arm. "What do I have to do?"

He allowed himself a second to narrow his eyes at Cliff before letting go of his shirt and facing me. "You need to put those clothes on. Since—"

"Guys, watch out!" I grabbed Whistler's hand and jerked him out of the way as the crocodile out of the pool snapped at us. Sheridan and Cliff were forced to the opposite corner of the room.

As it headed toward Whistler and me, I got a clear look at it. Unlike a crocodile, its talons and feet were webbed, more like an alligator, and the stinger at the tip of its tail was part of a large fanlike fin. It used it for balance as it reared and clawed at us like a grizzly bear, its snakelike tongue as long and wide as a girth strap on a western saddle.

A couple crocs in the pool closed in on Sheridan and Cliff, but the rest (that weren't still occupied with the exit) swam toward Whistler and me, apparently strategizing.

"Is there a knife in your backpack?" I asked. We leapt out of the way as the croc by the pool slammed down, inches away from the wall.

With no time to dig through a backpack, he glanced hesitantly at the shallow side and then looked at me. "Keep your mouth closed tight, and try to keep your head tilted up. This stuff could splash up."

Before the crocs could block our path, Whistler grabbed my hand and pulled me into the poison, which reached my knees. For a moment, I feared it would sting our skin or something—poison in Post World may not have been typical—but it was deceptively cool and smooth as it flowed under my jeans.

The champagne-colored liquid sloshed and leapt up around us as we bounded across the shallow side of the pool. I winced, my lips pressed together, as a drop touched my jaw. Strangely, it didn't stick, just rolled off my skin as if it were plastic or glass.

Whistler kept glancing at me as we ran, and I glanced back at the guys, who'd distracted a couple more crocodiles. I didn't know how long they could dodge them.

As we neared the square of dry floor, Whistler dared to speak, slowing a little so the poison wouldn't slosh as high. "Since only a female descendant of Selket can return artifacts to Post World, I'm guessing that only a descendant of Selket can tame the crocodiles, one who resembles her."

I nodded. Though I was skeptical, that was the only thing anyone had thought of that made sense.

Finally, Whistler jumped onto the dry floor. I winced as I stumbled, afraid of falling face first into the poison, but he pulled me up behind him. Not even daring to pause for a deep breath, I stripped my sweater, tennis shoes and jeans, only vaguely aware that I was in a room with three guys. They could see through clothes if they wanted, anyway, so it didn't matter. Whistler kept his eyes up as he handed me the bundle of clothes, and I knew he would have done that even if I hadn't been stripping for our lives right now.

The crocodiles in front of them, I couldn't see Cliff and Sheridan, but when they screamed, I hurriedly stepped into the long, gold skirt and gold half-top. I was about to shout at the crocodiles when Whistler stopped me and fastened a turquoise and amethyst collar around my neck and then a gold headdress around my forehead and hair.

"Wait," he said, stopping me again. Gingerly, he took the bandages off my face and the ponytail holder out of my hair. Getting the message, I made sure nothing else showed that wasn't Egyptian, taking off my socks before glancing at Whistler for courage.

I shouted at the crocodiles just as Sheridan and Cliff screamed again. The majority at the far end of the pool paid me no mind, but the two that had lingered by the exit the whole time turned and drifted toward me.

As they neared, their pace slowed, eyes calm. I swallowed hard. They stopped by the divider that separated the nearest shallow side from the main pool. My hands shaking, I glanced at Whistler, whose eyes echoed my fear.

Taking a deep breath, I took a step toward one of the crocodiles. When it didn't move, I took another, then another, until I stepped over its head and onto its back.

As I faced Whistler, it backed up in the venom. The combined motions blurred my vision, my head injuries throwing me off balance. I swayed a little before crouching and grabbing onto the raised scales on the crocodile's back, fighting off threats of nausea.

When Whistler tried to step onto the same crocodile, it and the other crocodile hissed at him, but made no move to attack. They were defending me now. He'd been right. They thought I was Selket.

Were these her actual clothes?

On the other side of the pool, there were more screams, followed by a splash this time. I thought I heard, "Selk, he's bleeding!" I couldn't tell who'd said it. Glancing over my shoulder, I saw the crocodiles in the venom and a figure struggling to stay afloat. I recognized Cliff's outline on the shore. He was crouched at the edge, extending his hand toward Sheridan, but the crocodiles blocked him.

Unsure of how to get my crocodile to carry me to them, I twisted to look at them better. When I did, the crocodile turned and swam in that direction. Panicked, I looked back at Whistler and held my hand out to him.

The other crocodile must have realized that he was with me. It remained calm as he took my hand and jumped onto my crocodile before it swam too far away from the square of dry floor.

Behind me, he sat on his knees and wrapped his arms around my waist to keep me steady.

The second crocodile followed us across the pool and swam in a circle around the group that had crowded around Sheridan. I gasped at the red expanding in the clear venom like a detonation. How much could the amulet power heal?

As soon as the other crocodiles saw Whistler and me, they must have realized Cliff and Sheridan were with me too. One of them swam below Sheridan and lifted him onto its back while the others backed away.

"Cliff, they're tamed," I said quietly. "Step aboard." He nodded, and after brief hesitation, stepped onto the nearest crocodile.

As the beasts carried us across the pool, I clutched Whistler's hands around my waist and said a prayer for Sheridan, who lay bloody and unconscious. He deserved way more credit than I'd given him.

A tear rolled down my face as the crocodile carrying Whistler and I approached the cramped tunnel of an exit. Just as I began to plan how we would drag Sheridan through such a narrow space, I met a pair of unfamiliar eyes, their owner a male—wearing gold.

Even when the crocodile bumped its nose on the edge of the pool, the amulet thief didn't move. The Egyptian garb or coffee skin wasn't what gave him away. It was his youth, that famous youth, that brought his name to my mind.

"Tutankhamen?"

CHAPTER TEN

Multiple Stories

He said nothing, just reached out to me. I couldn't turn to face Whistler, so I just squeezed his hands, and he squeezed mine back. How was he there? Animate mummies were one thing, but the real Tutankhamen? If it wasn't him, he had a twin.

Seeing my hesitation, he said something in Arabic, then showed us the amulet before placing it around his neck.

For a moment, I struggled to remember how to say, "I don't speak Arabic very well," in Arabic. Wishing I'd studied it as a second language rather than picking up a few words and phrases through Egyptology sites, I said, hoping I was right, "*Anaa la 'atakallam al-xarabiyya jayyidan.*"

Tutankhamen averted his eyes in thought, then replied, "Hal tatakallam 'inglizi?"

The words sounded familiar, especially the last one. I knew I'd read them somewhere before, or maybe heard them on an archaeological video. The last word registered.

"English," I said, astonished that he'd heard of the relatively recent language. "Yes, I speak English. We all do." As he glanced at the crocodiles, I wondered how he'd managed to make it past them, but didn't have time to ask. Sheridan was hurt badly.

"Can you help my friend?" I pressed. "The venom entered his veins. We need to get him to a safe place."

Tutankhamen looked at Sheridan, then back to me. "You have made peace with crocodiles," he said, the clarity of his English taking me aback. "We must cross pool. We cannot drag through tunnel ahead. Too narrow."

My eyes widened. He really expected us to stay in a room filled with venom, poison and crocodiles? "How long will the crocodiles ignore us?"

"While you look like Selket and I look like Tutankhamen."

I glanced at my gold outfit, then at his. *Look* like? Was this the real Tut or just an imposter like me?

He stepped onto the back of a vacant crocodile. I shifted my torso a little, directing my crocodile back to the other side of the pool. Once we all stepped onto dry ground, Tut helped the guys take off Sheridan's (my) backpack and drag him to the entrance of the venom pool, nearly back into the palace hall.

I had endless questions for Tut—or the imposter—but the only thing that mattered now was that he seemed to want to help us. The pool had washed away some of the blood, but the ripped sleeve on Sheridan's right arm was dark red and drying. I walked closer.

"Is he of Selket's blood?" Tut asked as I approached.

"No," I said. "He absorbed power from the amulet to enter Post World. I'm the only descendent of Selket here." *Unless you are too.*

The urgency left Tut's face, and he stood, leaving Cliff and Whistler crouched by Sheridan. "He will be fine," he said. "He heals now as he sleeps."

I sighed, relieved. "There's nothing else we can do for him?"

"No," Tut said, then gestured for Cliff, Whistler and me to follow him. "As he sleeps, we must talk."

"Where are you going?" I asked.

He stopped, emerald shadows reflecting off his thin, bare chest. "We must not awaken him."

Nodding, I followed him a little way into the palace hall, Cliff and Whistler behind me. All of us were too wound up to sit down.

"Why have you been avoiding us all this time?" I glanced at Tut's neck. "Why did you steal the amulet?"

"I needed your assistance," Tut said. "Over years, centuries, I have been to worlds of many guardians, even my own. Still, I cannot find my Drusilla."

I furrowed my brows. "Your *own* world? Centuries?" Taken aback, I pressed, "You're a guardian? How? I thought only those gifted with power could be guardians."

"And who's Drusilla?" Cliff added.

"You are right, Selk," Tut said. "I will explain."

"How do you know my name?"

Tut leaned against the wall. "I heard all of you say each other's names as you followed me here." He addressed each of us correctly. "Whistler, Cliff. Sheridan is sleeping one."

"Thanks for the clues," Whistler said, "but why didn't you approach us to begin with? If you needed help, we would have helped you."

"I could not know that," Tut said. "Descendants are urgent to leave. Most barely acknowledge me. While you listen, I beg you. I will help you leave this world if you help me leave with you so I may find my Drusilla of Mauretania, daughter of Cleopatra Selene, granddaughter of Cleopatra." He looked at Whistler and me, bona fide desperation in his eyes. "She is mine love. Like you both. You must understand."

I didn't know what shocked me more—that the *real* Tutankhamen was talking to us, that he was in love with a girl—Cleopatra's granddaughter—born centuries after his time, or that even a millennia-old pharaoh had seen how much I loved Whistler and, apparently, how much Whistler loved me.

Out of my peripheral vision, I saw Cliff glare at Tut. Whistler looked at me, but I didn't dare to look at him. Tut may have called us out on our feelings, but we hadn't told each other yet. And what if Tut was wrong about Whistler?

I pushed those thoughts to the back of my mind. This wasn't the right time.

Nodding at Tut, I said, "That sounds fair enough, but you'll have to tell us everything."

"I requested for Selket to guard my palace once," he began. "She didn't stay long, but did her job well. In that time, she saved many of my people from stings of scorpions and bites of serpents and other dreaded creatures from desert. In that small time, she saw my blessings—my wife, my children, my reign. And she saw that still I was not happy.

"When my brother, a year younger than myself, died, Selket saw opportunity I otherwise would not have seen because of grief. My brother resembled me much. And so, with Selket's help, my people thought they buried me."

I gaped at him, unable to say anything. Everything I'd studied about him. Everything the *world* had studied about him. And he'd changed it in seconds.

"I loved my wife," he continued, "and my children. And Egypt. It wasn't enough. So I accepted Selket's help and fled Egypt, traveling to many countries. She guided me for some time before making me a guardian and giving me my own world. It wasn't until after I realized she'd given me her own power and immortality that I knew, in a way, I was deceived. As I, she no longer wanted responsibility."

Staring at the floor, he laughed once, and said, "She died but a few years later by a scorpion of all things, leaving me with immortality, a millennium to wander countries before I returned to Egypt and met Drusilla." He closed his eyes. "Her hair was like sun, and her eyes like sky and her skin like clouds. And she was clever like first Cleopatra, as I heard."

Pain filled his eyes. "We loved immensely, but she grew ill by drinking harmful water. I could not save her life, I could not give her immortality already given to me. Nut, last original guardian, lived at palace of second Cleopatra Selene. She gladly gave up her immortality.

"I knew this later. I kissed my Drusilla and left, but when I found out she was well, I returned, but she was gone. Nut told me she had retreated to her world, thinking I had abandoned her. So I entered both Nut's and Drusilla's worlds, but she was not there. I have searched every world, including my own, but have not found her. She must be alive still. She must. She cannot give up her immortality." The desperation spread from his eyes to his voice. He beat the wall with his palm, red pigment on his fingertips.

"Maybe she's looking for you too," I said, horrified by the thought of never seeing Whistler again. "If you've traveled through all of the guardians' worlds, why can't you leave Selket's?"

"Because, although I do not have her healing abilities, I carry her power," he said. "Crocodiles know it, which is why they will not attack me, though only you can fully tame them. And though I have my own world, this one knows I carry Selket's power and it won't let me leave. Only Selket herself can take me with her to another world, but she is dead, so only a descendant may help me now." Glancing at me, he added, "Selket's power tells me this artifact is last. You are my last chance."

I leaned against the wall, processing the information. I was grateful he wanted to help, but this complicated things so much more. And I couldn't get over the fact that there were as many immortals walking around on Earth now as there had been original Egyptian guardians millennia ago.

"We'll help you," Cliff said, surprising me, then added under his breath, "I know how hard it is, not being able to be with the girl you love."

Whistler must have heard him, because he spoke next. "Do you know where to return the amulet?"

"Yes," Tut said. "I would have returned it myself, but even Selket herself could not have returned it. Only a female *descendent.*"

"Well, where?" I pressed, sympathetic but growing impatient.

"What resembles Horus' temple in this world."

Feeling sick, I exchanged glances with Whistler and Cliff, and knew all three of us wanted to strangle Tut.

Taking a step toward him, I growled, "You have got to be kidding. Why did you make us go through all this? We could have *all* been out of here hours ago!"

"I needed to learn about all of you, to ensure I could trust you. As I said, you are my last chance. Even immortal, I was outnumbered. You would have reclaimed amulet and left me behind before I had chance to plead for help."

"We couldn't have done that," Whistler countered. "We didn't know where to return it. And still don't exactly."

"In what would have been my sarcophagus," Tut said. "This amulet was taken from my brother's tomb, which Selket briefly looked after."

"So that's why the lid was open," I said, my voice softer.

"I planned to tell you then, but I had to be sure of you. Now I have no choice but to trust you." He looked at us with an expression that added, *Can I trust you?*

"Don't worry. We'll help you." Taking a deep breath, I said, "I don't know how long you've been stuck here, but I'm sure you know the labyrinth like the back of your hand. I presume that's the fastest way back to the Temple of Horus." I was not facing the mummies again.

"Because I know it, yes," Tut confirmed. "We will continue once Sheridan has healed."

We all stood in silence for a moment, processing everything. Whistler touched my hand once, but drew back before taking it. His face was unreadable, lost in thought. I swallowed hard. Had what Tut said upset him? Was he afraid we'd rushed into things?

Probably sensing the change of mood, Tut said, "You all should rest. I will sit with crocodiles."

"I'll sit with Sheridan in case he wakes up," Cliff said, throwing me a glance that told me he didn't trust Tut and still didn't trust Whistler.

Thinking out loud once Tut and Cliff were out of earshot, I turned to Whistler, and asked, "Should I trust you?"

He furrowed his brows, taken aback. "What do you mean?"

"That look on your face a moment ago." Averting my eyes, I fiddled with the smooth fabric of my gold skirt, and murmured, "You looked like you were considering breaking my heart."

"Breaking *your* heart?" When I looked at him, he laughed once and ran a nervous hand through his hair. "A thousands-year-old pharaoh just called me out. It scared me because he read my mind."

"He did?"

"Yeah." Whistler kept my gaze as he closed the distance between us. "It's fast, I know, but…I love you, Selk. And I'm terrified, because I don't know if you love me back yet, or if you ever will."

Inside, I leaped with glee, but I was sure my face didn't reflect that. I gaped at him. "I guess we don't have as much in common as I thought." I couldn't stifle a smile when utter terror filled his face. "How could we?" I continued. "We're obviously not going to be one of those couples who can read each other's minds."

I turned my back to him to bite back a grin, then spun into his arms and kissed him for a while.

My forehead against his, I said, wishing that everyone could hear, "I love you." Now I knew true love existed. How else could I have fallen for a boxer who'd been born in Croatia, raised by my Egyptian grandparents in the United States and made a Cyclops by one of their artifacts, which was up to me to return?

"You know," he murmured, "you look great in gold."

I glanced down, having forgotten I'd hastily changed clothes. "That's good, because unless the poison rolls off my jeans like it did our skin, I'm stuck in this until we get back to Egypt." I shivered, the unnaturally cool air of Post World brushing my bare arms and stomach.

Whistler took off his hoodie and draped it over my shoulders, leaving nothing but the t-shirt he wore underneath.

My voice soft, I asked, "What made you kiss me the first time?"

He smiled a small smile. "I remembered what you said about people being jerks."

"You said it first."

"I *believed* you." He brushed his fingers against my jaw. "You opened my eyes, Selk, and I want to thank you for that."

* * * *

It only took an hour for Sheridan to sleep off the venom. Fortunately, between the three backpacks, there were a couple spare shirts and pairs of pants (more fortunately, the backpacks were waterproof). I considered taking the other shirt, but Whistler insisted he didn't need his hoodie back, and wearing it kept my butterflies busy.

We each swallowed an energy bar (the first thing Tut had eaten in decades), and before we all discussed the labyrinth, I took back my I'd-rather-hug-a-mummy remark and gave Sheridan a hug.

"What was that for?" he asked, Cliff unsuccessfully hiding an amused smile.

"You didn't have to come here," I said. "Thank you."

He winked. "You look good in gold."

Despite wanting to punch him, I couldn't help but laugh and exchange glances with Whistler.

Standing at the edge of the venom pool, Tut looked nervously at the exit on the other side. "My last chance to find my Drusilla," he murmured, then turned to us. "Are you all ready?"

We'd filled Sheridan in on Tut, but hadn't discussed the labyrinth. With Tut knowing the way, we assumed we wouldn't need a plan, except to stick together, which had pretty much been our only one all along.

We all nodded, but when the crocodiles turned around at our approach, they hissed and reared up on their tails, the venom splashing around them.

I panicked for a moment before realizing what was wrong, then gave Whistler's hoodie back to him. "I never knew crocodiles were so opinionated on ancient fashion."

We stood on the crocodiles' backs this time as they carried us across the pool, Whistler's arms around my waist. Tut crawled into the dark tunnel first, and Sheridan followed, barely able to fit. I could hardly see in front of me. *Why couldn't some of the descendants have installed lanterns or something in this place?*

We crawled for at least ten minutes before the tunnel opened and things were fully visible again. Too visible. Everything was too bright. I squinted at the rainbow of waving glows, wondering if we were still in the same world until I recognized characteristics of Egyptian architecture.

Yet the labyrinth there was nothing like the illustrations I'd seen. Instead of white marble, as Herodotus had described, the endless columns, ceiling, floors and vast walls that surrounded us were stained glass. And rather than two stories, the building was as tall as four.

"I thought structures here are supposed to be smaller than what they are in Egypt," I commented, standing.

"This is smaller," Tut said, moving through the multi-colored light toward the entrance.

Trancclike, I followed him, the glowing glass cold beneath my bare feet. This was by far the most beautiful site in Selket's Post World.

"How can we go through a maze," I began, "that has multiple stories?"

Tut smiled over his shoulder. "You follow me."

I was relieved that Tut seemed to know what he was doing and where he was going. Who knew how long it would have taken to decipher a drawing of a four-story labyrinth in the guidebook.

"Be wary," he added. "Outside is dead. Inside, labyrinth sleeps."

"Sleeps?" I furrowed my brows at the still structure. "So these columns will swing too, if we walk by them?"

"No," Tut clarified. "There are many movements. I will warn you as we approach. To explain them all now would confuse and take time."

I paused, waiting for the guys behind me to catch up, who were still taking in the vast, gorgeous structure.

"I will warn you of this," Tut added as Whistler took my hand. "Changeless glowing glass can confuse. You must be careful to move slowly when possible."

"So it's pretty much like a funhouse," Cliff concluded, though I was certain Tutankhamen had no clue what that was.

"In Egypt," Tut said, either ignoring Cliff or not hearing him, "Selket favored labyrinth." Stopping, he looked at me, and added, "She also died there."

My skin prickled, but the creepy words were pushed to the back of my mind when Tut walked to Whistler and fiddled with the zipper on his hoodie.

Whistler's eyes widened, but he didn't say anything, just exchanged a freaked-out glance with me.

"What are you doing?" I asked for him.

Giving up, Tut stepped back, and said, pointing at Whistler's hoodie, "Give that back to her. Crocodiles could only be tamed by Selket. However, I do not know how this labyrinth will react."

Whistler nodded and unzipped his hoodie, then I zipped it up on me, glad to have it back. I so knew what I was getting Whistler for his birthday, because something told me I'd accidentally forget to return this one.

Cliff, annoyed, caught up to Tut, and they talked about something I couldn't hear as we approached the expansive entrance. As they waited for us before stepping inside, the pharaoh even placed his hand on Cliff's shoulder as if offering sympathy for something, a gesture I wasn't sure had been used often in ancient Egypt.

"...like Drusilla," Tut said as I neared.

After seeing the understanding on Sheridan's face, I realized what was going on. Cliff empathized with Tut because of Drusilla. Because of me. Tut couldn't be with his girl. I wasn't Cliff's and I never had been, but...

I took a deep breath, trying to concentrate on what lay ahead. Maybe Drusilla had an immortal cousin I could introduce Cliff to once we got out of there. I had to find him someone to make him forget about the idea of us. Knowing that I caused him so much grief was torment.

CHAPTER ELEVEN

Going Out

The first story of the labyrinth was bare and vast. Tut had explained that nothing would move on this level. I still wasn't sure of when or where they would, but I trusted his judgment. He'd helped us with Sheridan, after all.

Of all the sites in Post World, this was the most peaceful. We'd been walking for about twenty minutes through a meadow-sized hall of glowing multi-colored glass when I realized my mind had drifted. Whistler was the only one in sight.

"Where'd they go?" I asked, hoping they'd stepped behind a wide column, but the many glowing hues made it hard to distinguish anything.

Before we could shout for them, I heard Tut call from ahead, "Keep up! We must not become separated!"

Exhaling in relief, I ran toward his voice, and Whistler followed. I nearly bumped into the young pharaoh when he stepped from behind a wall.

"Stay closer," he warned. "Sameness is dangerous. Even with a map, you could not find your way out of labyrinth."

We followed Tut around the corner, where Cliff and Sheridan waited, and continued down a narrow passage that turned constantly. Though we all stayed close together, we kept having to stop for one or two of us to catch up. All of us (even Tut) bumped into glowing glass way too many times, thinking it was empty space.

Once the turns stopped, we approached a staircase of some sort. The steps were shaped like crocodiles.

"This isn't where the labyrinth wakes up, is it?" I asked, wary.

"No," Tut said. "Staircase never wakes, because it does not sleep. Next story will awaken, as well as last two."

Slowly, but confidently, we climbed the glowing crocodile staircase to the next level, a hall of seemingly endless rooms, each open like a museum display. The colors and glass were the same, but the shapes were different— statues and pottery and jewelry and other artifacts, arranged specifically in each room.

"I searched every room here for my Drusilla," Tut said as we admired the hall. "After that, I knew she must be on Earth. Perhaps in Egypt." Cliff was about to comment, but Tut cut him off. "Be still, my friends," he said, holding up a hand to stop us. "Ahead, they will awaken."

"'They?'" I repeated.

"Crocodiles," he explained.

"I thought there were no more crocodiles," I said.

"There are no more that can be tamed." He added, "We are approaching many rooms to our right that are tombs of mummified crocodiles."

"Mummies?" I whispered, my throat dry. "Do they carry their sarcophaguses too?"

"Yes."

The glowing glass blurred. I grabbed Whistler's hand, struggling to keep from passing out.

"Selk?" He wrapped an arm around my waist.

"Maybe they won't be as bad," I said, though my voice shook.

"They cannot slow you," Tut confirmed. I felt better until he said, "They do not need to. Once they awaken, we must run."

Though I couldn't stop a whimper, I refused to cower against my boyfriend's shoulder. I'd made peace with crocodiles. They wouldn't scare me, mummified or not.

Slowly, we walked past the rooms where the crocodiles slept. Unlike the stairs, their sarcophaguses nearly blended into the glowing glass. I braced myself when I heard an echoing thud, but it'd just been Sheridan stumbling on the speedbump-like divider I'd just stepped over.

When I heard a similar noise, I kept walking with the others, but my stomach tensed. In Khafre, the sarcophaguses had opened in the middle of the floor. And I'd never known a divider to be in a hallway.

"Guys," I whispered without turning around, "it's time to run."

Tut glanced over his shoulder. I must have been right, because he broke into a sprint. As we followed him, I heard glass crashing against glass behind us, but not shattering.

The same length we'd walked on the first floor, we ran on the second, the number of crocodiles following increasing.

"They won't follow us to next floor," Tut called.

I glanced at the crocodiles, who looked as if they should have been tripping over their own bandages or at least slowed by the sarcophaguses on their backs. "How do we get to the next floor?" I asked, the crocodiles gaining on us.

"Ladder," Tut said.

Instead of running to the end of the hall as I'd expected, Tut ducked into a room on the right and then climbed the wide ladder that stood in the middle. I looked up, but couldn't see where it ended because of the glow.

"Tutankhamen." The voice was so faint I thought it was a whisper at first, but when it spoke again, I realized it was a muffled shout.

"Selk, come!" Tut grabbed my wrist and yanked me up the ladder behind him, the guys following me.

"I—"

"Come!" he repeated, letting go of my wrist so he could climb faster.

Luckily, the ladder wasn't too long. As Cliff, the last of the group, climbed onto the new floor, I peered at the lower level. My eyes widened. The crocodiles, without their sarcophaguses, were actually climbing the ladder.

"They must sense amulet," Tut said. "They never follow this far."

"I heard a voice," I blurted. "It said your name, Tut. That's what I was trying to tell you down there."

He whirled toward me. "A voice? What did it sound like?"

I bit my lip, thinking hard. "I guess soft, maybe female. I couldn't really tell. It was muffled."

Tut gasped, then peered back at the ladder. The first crocodile had climbed over halfway.

"We need to go," Sheridan said.

"Tut, man, come on," Cliff pressed. "We don't know the way."

All Tut could say, whisper, was, "My Drusilla…"

"If she's down there," Sheridan said, "you won't be able to get to her. There are too many crocodiles."

"Drusilla," Tut repeated, not hearing him.

It had to be her. She'd been there all this time, and now we knew why Tut hadn't been able to find her—a crocodile had shut her in its sarcophagus like the mummy had shut me in. Only she couldn't die. She'd lived for who knew how many years in there, probably calling to Tutankhamen whenever he'd run past. Yet he'd never heard her, because he'd always climbed the ladder too quickly.

He turned to us, his face filled with desperation. "You must help me. I beg you. I cannot free her on my own."

"The crocodiles..." Cliff protested.

He was right. One by one, they kept climbing the ladder. And if we didn't start running soon, they'd catch up and kill us all, except Tut.

If we started running now...

"The crocodiles are following us," I said, "and leaving their sarcophaguses behind. That means Drusilla will be or has already been freed. If we go back, we'll drive the crocodiles back, risking one capturing her again."

Tut's face fell, but he didn't protest. Instead, he said, "Come," and took off running.

With a sigh of relief, I followed him and glanced at Whistler, imagining how I'd feel if he'd been down there instead of Drusilla.

This story was a curvy maze, artifacts blending with the stained-glass architecture. The endless turns both worked to our advantage and against us—we were always out of the crocodiles' sights, but we never knew which way we'd be turning. There were so many curves at one point I felt as if I were a snake and the labyrinth my charmer. After running into a fourth wall, I felt my way to avoid more collisions.

I kept losing the guys. Every other turn, Tut would disappear for a few seconds, and by the time he came into sight again, I'd glance behind me, and Whistler, Cliff and Sheridan would be gone.

At first, I didn't notice the tilt in the floor, but as we ran, I found myself leaning to the right. My shoulder rubbed the wavy wall and my ankles protested as my feet tried to run on the slanting surface.

Tut came to a stop.

"Tut," I said, glancing toward the hisses of the approaching crocodiles, "we need to keep running." When I looked back, I saw him gaping and what had caused him to gape. Though wavy like the rest of the story, the wall in front of us was solid.

"Do not worry," he said. "Labyrinth is awakening."

Seconds after he said that, the waves in the walls rolled like a snake, throwing us off balance. The guys and I crashed into the opposite wall, but before we could regain our footing, the floor and ceiling rolled as well. Soon the entire winding hall rolled, tossing us around like names shuffled in a hat.

"How can this help us?" I shouted before falling against a wall.

"Crocodiles cannot catch us now," he said. "And we will be at next level soon."

"Then why did you act so surprised?" Whistler asked.

"I do not remember that wall. My sarcophagus must sense amulet and know I stole it from Selket's descendent, even from here. Post World is reacting."

"By blocking us in?" Cliff pressed, leaping over a curve. "How do we get out of here?"

Tut was about to reply when a crocodile, snapping and bandaged, came sliding toward us, followed by several more. The hall—maybe the entire labyrinth—turned upside down. I braced myself for the impact, for the crushing weight and jaws of the crocodiles. The guys and I just fell and fell, the crocodiles falling with us. It was as if I were back in an airplane, watching the landscape from the sky.

We fell away from a huge maze of columns. Though the walls didn't move this time, the floor still rolled up and down, and artifacts leapt around.

"The exit!" Sheridan shouted.

I looked where he pointed and could just make out a small dark spot, the only one that didn't glow or move. It had to be another tunnel or passageway, and it was to the back right of the maze.

The farther we fell, the more my thoughts drifted from getting out of there. If we landed on the glass wall that encompassed the labyrinth, even with the guys' healing abilities, I knew only Tut would survive.

"Tut!" I screamed. "The glass! What do we do?"

When Tut managed to throw me a glance that told me he honestly didn't know, I closed my eyes and braced myself for death. After everything, glass would kill us.

As blood rushed to my feet and my stomach dropped as if I were riding an upside-down roller coaster, I opened my eyes again. The labyrinth was righting itself, the main wall tilting gradually as we fell toward the maze.

It hurt to hit the glass, but it was a heck of a lot better than cracking open my skull. We slid down the wall, involuntarily following the crocodiles. Luckily, they'd fallen farther to the left than we had, and when we finally landed, the guys and I were separated from them by a divider of columns.

There was no time to think about regaining our footing. We just had to. Whistler found my hand and pulled me across the waving floor, and we dodged the glass artifacts that leapt from the columns. Ahead, Cliff and Sheridan punched and kicked things that flew into their paths, but Tut just kept running, pummeled or not. I knew he only had one thing, one person, on his mind, and admired his determination.

"Guys, the exit," I said, my stomach tensing. "I lost track of its direction when I fell, but I know we landed near it."

"We're going the right way," Sheridan said. "I can see it."

Panting, I glanced over my shoulder. The crocodiles had almost caught up to us. I'd never seen crocodiles, especially mummified ones, run so fast.

Before I could warn the guys, the exit came into view. We bolted toward it. With no time to search for flashlights, we felt our way through pitch blackness. I couldn't tell how wide or tall the passage was, or what was inside. There were thuds and clanks and hisses and muffled screams. I clutched Whistler's hand tighter.

"Guys, are you still here?" I called.

"Yeah," Cliff said.

"Just run!" Sheridan added.

Something metal crashed into me, like a plate, breaking apart Whistler's and my hands. I felt for him in the darkness, relieved when a warm hand grasped mine, and kept running as more metal things collided with me.

I screamed when something snapped at my heels, accompanied by a hiss. "The crocodiles!" I shouted, gripping Whistler's hand tighter.

Once we finally left the tunnel and found ourselves back in Horus' temple, it wasn't Whistler's hand I held—it was Cliff's. Panicked, I pulled mine away and ran faster, searching until I found Whistler, who ran a few feet ahead with Tut and Sheridan. Cliff glared but didn't break stride as Whistler slowed to reclaim my hand.

Artifacts rained on us as we ran, and a few yards from Tut's imitation tomb, a couple columns dropped from the ceiling. We all fell to the floor to dodge them, but that was only the beginning of our hindrances.

"What's going on?" I asked.

"Post World is celebrating last artifact...artifact...artifact..."

I gasped as Tut's voice morphed to echoes, and soon all of us were breathing and crawling in slow motion. Far away, the mummies came into view, and though the swinging columns had slowed the mummified crocodiles behind us, their hisses grew louder.

The floor changed to stained glass and rolled, pushing us both backward and forward in our slow motion. When a shallow sheet of swirled venom and poison leaked from below us, I kept my mouth closed, though my whimper echoed as the emerald-colored crocodiles from the pool passed the mummies heading toward us.

The crocodiles...

I had no idea how or if we would get to Tut's sarcophagus, but having one less thing against us, maybe something for us, would help.

Finally out of range of the columns, the guys and I struggled to stand, and gradually, I unzipped and slipped out of Whistler's hoodie. Immediately, the crocodiles in front of us slowed. Some of them turned on the mummies, while the rest charged past us toward the mummified crocodiles.

The mummies distracted, we moved quickly again. "Tut, the amulet!" I called.

He took it off his neck and then handed it to me as we ducked into his imitation tomb, which, thankfully, was calm. The eye glowed as I approached the sarcophagus. Glancing at Cliff, Sheridan and Whistler, I saw that their Cyclops eyes had appeared. I took a deep breath, afraid it wouldn't work, and pushed the lid off the sarcophagus.

"Wait," Tut said, clasping his hand around the amulet. "You must wait for my Drusilla. Crocodiles from labyrinth are distracted."

I hesitated, not wanting to leave anyone behind, but also not wanting things to go wrong and us all to be trapped there.

Before I could speak, Sheridan said, "We don't have time, man."

Tut stared at us for a long moment, then nodded at us and took off toward the swinging columns. I understood—if he found her before we'd all left Post World, he would come with us. If not, he would stay there and not hold a grudge, because regardless, he'd have his Drusilla.

I bit my lip, praying she'd followed the mummified crocodiles there. I returned my attention to the sarcophagus.

As I dropped the amulet in, it lit the coffin's interior, and the guys' Cyclops eyes glowed brighter, reminding me we had three more to go.

Sheridan touched the amulet first, then Cliff. Their third eyes vanished for good. I held my breath as Whistler did the same, wondering where the portal would appear, hoping it would appear at all.

Just when I feared there was some special thing I'd have to do, it showed up right on the wall in front of us, covering half of the chalky painting Tut had done of Drusilla. Clear unlike the first time it had opened, I wanted to cry when I saw the sky of Egypt through the entrance to the real Temple of Horus. I was even more relieved when I realized it was early night and no one would be around to question us.

I may have been too inexperienced to learn how to tell which artifacts were missing from Post World or where to return them, but the moment the portal had appeared, a complete peace filled me, letting me know this was the end. For all of Selket's descendants.

I glanced at the portal, hesitating, then glanced toward the columns and mummified crocodiles. No sign of Tut.

No sign of the emerald-colored crocodiles either.

"Guys," I said, "I don't see the crocodiles. Did they go after Tut? Should we wait for him?" Before any of them could answer, I glanced back toward the mummies, but didn't see them. The crocodiles that had been holding them off blocked them from view, rearing on their tails.

"Selk, run!" Cliff shouted, grabbing my arm and yanking me toward the portal. Sheridan followed, but Whistler didn't act quickly enough, and the mummies, working with the crocodiles now rather than against them, slowed his movements.

"Whistler!"

I screamed his name over and over, fighting to get to him, but Cliff pulled me back, and several crocodiles blocked my path as another one took Whistler between its teeth and reared. Even his screams of pain came out in slow echoes.

He called my name once, which echoed three times. I elbowed Cliff in the gut, freeing myself, but he grabbed me again before I could leap forward, pulling me backward through the portal this time.

As I fell, I saw Sheridan hesitate, but the crocodiles snapped at him, and he pulled my last hope of saving Whistler through the portal with him.

My screams were only interrupted briefly by the impact of falling into Egypt. Though I couldn't see Whistler, I could still see scales. I leapt to my feet and raced toward the portal, but Cliff and Sheridan both pulled me back this time. I punched, elbowed and kicked every body part of theirs I could reach, even ran a little way up a column in attempt to twist out of their grips via a backflip, but they were too strong.

"Whistler, no!" I screamed.

Even as I collapsed to my knees, I still struggled. Even as the portal closed, I struggled. After it disappeared, I threw myself on the ground and sobbed. And sobbed. And sobbed.

I didn't know how long I'd been crying when Cliff dared to lay a hand on my shoulder, but the moment he did, I whirled and decked his face. As he stumbled, I leapt to my feet and pummeled any part of him I could reach before Sheridan pulled me backward.

"How could you leave him there?" I shrieked, my vision blurred with tears. "How could you pull me away from him?"

"Selk, you would have died!" Cliff shouted. "None of us could have saved him!"

"You overprotective freak!" I roared, then thrashed left and right, trying to free myself from Sheridan's grip. I struggled and struggled until I swung myself into a nearby column and got a third concussion that finally knocked me out.

SITE FIVE: SNOW HILL, MARYLAND

CHAPTER TWELVE

After All

I'd never been in the hospital nearest Snow Hill. I hadn't wanted to go at all, but somehow, Cliff and Sheridan managed to track down Zahid, who'd gotten us out of Egypt and back to the States as quickly as possible. I'd slept most of the time, and the rest of it, I didn't really remember, because I'd been too numb.

I must have had enough energy to change airports and walk off planes, but I didn't remember much of it. Once I'd woken up in the hospital, Mom had told me I'd been there a week. And when I got home, I stayed there, sobbing, for another week before daring to peek outside.

The snow wasn't as deep as it had been when I'd left. I walked on the side of the street opposite Mack's and the gym, hoping to not run into anyone, especially Cliff. Of course it would be hard to walk down the street without seeing anyone I knew.

Especially Cliff.

My head down as I walked, I bumped right into him.

"Selk…" He kept his mouth open to say something else, but appeared as if he couldn't find any words.

"Cliff," I said, my voice quiet.

Clearing his throat, he finally managed, "'How are you?' is probably a stupid question."

"Incredibly stupid." I stared over his shoulder, willing him to get on with whatever he wanted to say.

"Selk, I'm sorry," he said. "Losing Whistler was awful, but if you'd been in my place, wouldn't you have done the same?"

"Probably," I muttered, still not meeting his gaze.

"It's still too soon, I know," he said, "but do you think you'll ever forgive me?"

I met his gaze then and thought about how easily Whistler had forgiven

Fadila and Naim, right before they'd betrayed him again. And I knew he would've forgiven Cliff. I knew he would've pulled me away too, had Cliff been the one trapped in Post World.

My voice trembling, I said, "Yeah."

His eyes tearing, he hugged me. "I love you, Selk," he said. "If you ever decide we could be right for each other, I'll be here. One year down the road, or ten."

"Cliff, it's not about our age difference. Even if I'd never met Whistler, it wouldn't have worked out between us. Don't wait. You deserve to make another girl happy. When you have everything, it's hard..." Crying now, I added, "You're amazing, Cliff, but a different kind of amazing. I just...I had everything..."

Cliff kept holding me as I sobbed. I cried for a few minutes before finally pulling back.

"I still don't understand. This is really insensitive, but..." Cliff wiped away one of my tears, then pressed his lips together. "What did you see in him? He was a jerk, he had no sense of humor, he wasn't as careful as he should have been regarding your safety, and he... This is really petty, but he wasn't even what most girls would call attractive."

I gaped at him, disgusted. "He was the complete *opposite* of that! Am I going to be the only one who knows what Whistler Aric Casebolt was truly like?" I didn't even have the strength to punch Cliff.

Instead, I bolted past him, sobbing again, and ran all the way to where I thought Sheridan's apartment complex was. I knocked on nine doors before I found him.

"Selk?"

The tears unending, I blurted, "I know he doesn't have any family or friends, so I was wondering...did you throw his stuff out yet?"

Sheridan smiled sadly. "No. I haven't touched his room."

I pushed past him and easily found Whistler's room in the small apartment. There wasn't much in it, and nothing unusual, just clothes and a bed and other things you'd expect to find in a college-aged guy's room.

I took the orange hoodie he'd worn to referee at Man Cave off his bed, put it on and zipped it up. "I know I'm probably asking in vain," I began, sniffling, "but do you remember seeing any pictures of him?"

Sheridan shook his head. "No, Selk. Sorry." He furrowed his brows, thinking hard. "Wait, there may be one small picture."

I held my breath as Sheridan found Whistler's wallet in a drawer, which he hadn't brought to Egypt. He pulled out his driver's license and handed it to me. I stared at the picture. He was younger there, but didn't look much different. When I saw the symbol for his being an organ donor, I burst into fresh tears, partly because no one could see how great of a guy he was, and partly because his body would never be found.

* * * *

The next week, I stayed wrapped in Whistler's hoodie, spending time with Mom and Tut. After that, Mom and I both forced me to go back to school, where I numbly told Brandie and Lynette that Whistler had died. I didn't tell them more than that. They wouldn't have believed me, and mostly, I didn't feel like explaining the paranormal details.

Thankfully, they didn't ask about Cliff.

Zahid, apparently, had disappeared again, and I didn't care. The last mentioning of him, though indirect, was an update on the Egyptology news page.

The Egyptology Gazette

Breaking News!

Return of Artifact

The stolen Eye of Horus amulet has been recovered! Last night, a cryptic man returned the amulet to the museum. Before any questions could be asked, he collected the promised reward and seemingly vanished. Where did he find it? Where did he go? One mystery is solved, only to leave another.

I scoffed at the article. Of course Zahid had found the amulet. Leaving Whistler behind was perfectly fine, but leaving an artifact was out of the question.

"Selk," Mom called from downstairs as I slammed my laptop shut, "have you finished your senior project?"

My stomach tensed. I'd watched the video of Whistler and I sparring until I knew it by heart.

"It's not due for a while," I replied. And I was grateful for that. I couldn't present that in front of my class right now. And I sure as heck wouldn't leave Whistler out when I did.

I heard Mom's footsteps on the stairs, and a few seconds later, my door opened. As Tut mewed at her approach, I wondered what had happened to the real Tutankhamen. I hoped he'd found his Drusilla.

"Selk…" Mom began, biting her lip. When I didn't say anything, she said, "Your birthday is in a few days. I understand if you don't want to, but your friends and I think you should get out, do something happy. Mack said you can have the whole restaurant that night, just a quiet celebration."

I just shrugged and averted my eyes. Mom sat on my bed and patted the arm of Whistler's hoodie, which mine was in. "He must have been some boy," she said.

"I'm going to love him forever." After a moment, I looked at Mom. "I'll go to Mack's as long as I can wear this."

She hugged me, appearing relieved.

* * * *

A few days later, everyone I'd expected to be at Mack's was there—Brandie, Lynette, Sheridan, Cliff, Mom and Mack himself, along with a few other people I was only acquainted with.

Having insisted on walking, I was late, and was greeted with two surprises. The first, Cliff talking and laughing with Mack's daughter, Martha, a tall, pretty blonde I'd only seen a few times because she'd been at college in another state. The second, Mom talking and laughing with Mack, his arm around her shoulders. I couldn't help but smile at that irony. Age really didn't matter.

After nodding at everyone and exchanging a solemn glance with Cliff, I sat by myself at a table in the corner and pulled Whistler's driver's license out of my pocket. We'd been so close. Only a few seconds sooner, and he would have been with me today, kissing me in front of everyone.

About halfway through what was supposed to be a party, Mom came and got me. At first, I thought it was to cut cake or something, but her gaze was serious. After following her glance at the door, I understood.

When he walked in, I bit my tongue and clenched my fists to keep from losing it. Though he wasn't directly to blame, he was close enough. And since I'd made peace with Cliff—though he still owed me an apology—I was left with Zahid.

I kept my gaze on the floor until he reached my table. "Hello, Selk."

"I thought you'd left again."

He shook his head. "I was taking care of some last-minute things." Of course. The amulet.

Which was why I was surprised when he said, "After everything, I'm low on money, so I wasn't able to buy you a gift."

I narrowed my eyes at him. "You really think I care about gifts right now?"

"I was able to bring you something."

He smiled at me before walking across the room and out the door. He was only gone for a few seconds before he stepped back inside. Though he didn't have anything in his hands, he grinned. I glanced at Mom, who looked as surprised as me.

A familiar young pharaoh walked in behind Zahid, a pretty redhead on his arm, both in modern clothes. Everyone in the room stopped and stared. My eyes filled with tears.

"They wanted to thank you," Zahid called from across the room.

"This never would have been possible without you," Tut added. "My greatest thanks, my dear Selk."

"I'm glad you guys found each other," I said, wiping a tear away. Everyone in the room was confused, save for Sheridan and Cliff, but I didn't care. Something had gone right.

Tut and Drusilla stepped into the room but didn't sit down. Zahid stared at the door, and they mimicked him.

Another young guy walked in, alone. Even when he pulled the hood down from his head, it didn't register. I blinked several times, and it still didn't register. He stared at me, and I stared at him. I pulled his hoodie tighter around me.

The shock morphing to urgency, I bolted from my chair, knocking it over. Grinning, he raced toward me, and we found each other in a collision in the middle of the room. He kissed me for a long while, then I sobbed into his hoodie, the one *he* wore.

"How?" I whispered, my voice choked with tears. "How?"

"Tut and Drusilla. Post World wanted to keep Tut because it sensed Selket's power, but Drusilla has Nut's power, so she was able to reopen the portal. Not having a fast-healing ability anymore sucks, but a few weeks in the hospital did the same job."

I mouthed "thank you" at Tut and Drusilla, then kissed Whistler again.

When someone—it sounded like Mack—yelled "happy birthday," I laughed and studied the astonished faces of those around me. Those who weren't close to me, like Mack's daughter, just smiled in a hopeless-romantic way.

I leaned in for another kiss when Whistler turned me back to him, but he stopped me, pinching the hoodie I wore. "You really missed me?" he asked.

"Are you kidding me?" When he stopped me from kissing him again, I furrowed my brows. "What's wrong?"

He smiled and took a small box out of his pocket. "This isn't a wedding ring, but…" He handed it to me, and inside I found an old-looking ring with multi-colored stones embedded the whole way around the dark metal. When I slipped it on, he added, "I remembered what we talked about, back in…" He glanced at everyone around us. "It's a promise ring instead of an engagement ring, because I want you to know how long I'm willing to wait for you."

Despite how happy I was, tears kept falling. He wiped some away.

Glancing at the hoodie I wore, I said, "I thought this was all I'd have left of you." I reached into my pocket, found his driver's license and handed it to him with a sniffle. "This is yours."

He blinked back tears of his own. "I missed you so much."

"Those were the longest weeks of my life," I whispered, leaning my forehead against his. "I hope you know how much I love you."

"I hope you know I would die for you."

"I do," I said. "I do."

He kissed me again, and murmured, "I love you, Selk."

I burrowed my face in his chest. I don't know how long we stayed like that, but I would have given anything to have spent the past few weeks like this. We had thousands of weeks to spend together, and now I didn't need thousands of weeks to truly forgive everyone I'd held a grudge against.

Now the only thing I held was the guy of my dreams.

EPILOGUE

Same Again

A year and a half later, I tripped several times on my way to the room in the back of the small church. Heels did not agree with me.

I'd gotten accepted into an Egyptology program in Tennessee, and a year after, so had Whistler, both of us having decided that we hadn't been scarred for life. We hadn't seen or heard from Tut and Drusilla since Snow Hill, but assumed they were off traveling the world, or Egypt, at least, probably getting used to the new millennium.

While waiting for the application season, Whistler started teaching boxing at a local gym (after adjusting to not being able to heal overnight anymore), where he taught advanced fighters. I taught beginners. It was weird, moving to the south and not seeing Cliff and Sheridan and the others every day. It was also amazing.

Now Whistler and I were back in Snow Hill for Cliff's wedding (much to Brandie's and Lynette's disappointment). I was so thankful he'd taken my advice on not waiting. He looked dashing in a tux, and Martha wore white beautifully.

After checking on her, I found Whistler, a groomsman, waiting by the doors to the chapel with the rest of the wedding party. He, Sheridan and Cliff had talked for a long time the night of my birthday at Mack's, and they'd kept in touch over phone and e-mail. I still couldn't believe it, but I didn't question it. Even Zahid, though disappointed that Mom had finally decided to move on with Mack, kept in touch. I knew he was proud of my college degree choice, and though I hated to admit it, that made me happy.

"You look beautiful," Whistler said, taking my arm.

I gave him a light kiss on the lips. "This'll probably be the only time we'll dress nice for a while, especially when we start field work in class."

"I'm excited for that."

"Really?"

"Yeah," he said. "I want to see what the *real* places we've already been to look like."

I laughed and was about to reply when Sheridan walked up. "Hey, you two," he said, gesturing at his tux. "What do you think? A good refereeing outfit?" He'd been promoted to full-time referee at Man Cave shortly after returning from Egypt.

"Better stick with best-man status for now," I said.

"Hey, guys." I turned at the sound of gel-haired Cliff's voice. "You ready?"

I grinned, taking a hand off Whistler's arm so I could reach out and adjust his tie. "Of course."

"Thank you for being here, guys," he said, then looked at me, "especially you, Selk."

It'd been a long time, but I knew he still thought about how many attempts he'd made to convince me to be with him. And I knew he'd always be ashamed of how he'd gone along with everyone and misjudged Whistler.

It was that shame that had made me truly forgive him.

I nodded at him, and he took a deep breath before opening the doors and then walking down the aisle. Though they hadn't been for a while, part of me was incredibly aware that things would never be the same again, that Cliff and I would never hang out at Man Cave on Friday nights again, that we wouldn't go to Mack's Shack after punching contests. Those times had been priceless, but what I had now, even more so.

Whistler squeezed my hand, and I held his arm tight so I wouldn't trip walking down the aisle. Sheridan, already in the best man spot, winked at me as Whistler and I went to the groomsman side.

"Whistler," I whispered as the music played, "whenever we get married, I don't want to get married in Egypt. Mummies might distort my speech when I tell you how much I love you in front of everyone."

He laughed, squeezing my hand. "We've still got a while before we go back to Egypt for class. And even when we do, I promise no more mummies will hurt you."

Unable to resist, I kissed him before Mack's daughter stepped into the chapel. I couldn't help but think about the domino effect Whistler had caused the first night I'd met him at Man Cave. I should have known then that I'd fall in love with him.

As I imagined the wedding crowd being jostled by him, brawling with Appleton, I stifled a laugh. He hadn't gotten into any more multiple-man fights, but I never got tired of watching him beat up a canvas bag.

And I never would.

* * * *

The day before…

Papers and clothes and who knew what crunched and crumpled as Cvijeta struggled to tidy her daughter's room. Selk and Whistler would be there tomorrow, leaving college for a few days to go to Cliff's wedding.

"I should make you clean it when you get here," she muttered, though she couldn't hide an affectionate smile. She'd gladly recycle thousands of trampled high-school essays, because her baby girl was safe, happy and had saved generations from the fear of early death.

After most of the floor was visible, Cvijeta moved on to the closet. Several items of clothing lay abused and forgotten. A gold, shimmery bundle tucked away in a half-open box caught her eye. She swallowed hard as she picked up each piece. It was the outfit Selk had worn out of Egypt, to the hospital in Snow Hill. The outfit she'd cried for her boyfriend in, who hadn't died, after all.

Cvijeta wiped away a tear and tucked the ancient ensemble back into the box. She knew how passionate her daughter was about Egyptology despite everything she'd been through, but after nearly two decades of fearing for Selk's life, she preferred not to think about it.

When the phone rang, she walked away and forgot about the skirt of flowing gold, the jeweled headdress and the other pieces.

"Okay, Selk. Love you. See you and Whistler tomorrow."

Cvijeta hung the phone up with a smile. She loved her job teaching art classes. She dreamed of one day helping Selk plan a wedding. Even sooner, she may have been planning her own wedding to possibly the kindest man she'd ever met. She fell into a peaceful sleep, giddy with how normal life had become.

* * * *

As Cvijeta dreamed, in the now-closed box in Selk's dark closet, gold light sparkled weakly, like a hostage screaming through a gag, then went out.

The End

ABOUT THE AUTHOR

After starting college at 16, Kristina M. Serrano graduated from Cape Fear Community College with an Associate's Degree in Arts, as well as a BFA in Creative Writing Fiction and a Certificate in Publishing from The University of North Carolina Wilmington, landing on the Dean's and Chancellor's lists. She was the Executive Editor and Prose Editor of an online literary magazine, and, while in college, had the privilege of singing The National Anthem at four large events. SLOW ECHOES is her first published novel, but she has dozens of unfinished YA fantasy and paranormal romance novels stored away for a rainy day. She currently resides in North Carolina with her hyper Bichon Frisé, Jake.

Visit Kristina's web site: www.kristinamserrano.wixsite.com/author

Like on Facebook: https://www.facebook.com/authorkristinamserrano

Follow on Twitter: https://twitter.com/booksandbichons

Follow on Tumblr: http://authorkristinamserrano.tumblr.com/